Beyond Our World

Book 1 – Stellar Soul

By David Rousseau

For permission, serialization, condensation, adaptations, or for our catalog of other publications, write to Ozark Mountain Publishing, Inc., P.O. box 754, Huntsville, AR 72740, ATTN: Permissions Department.

Library of Congress Cataloging-in-Publication Data
Rousseau, David – 1973-
Beyond Our World, Book 1 – Stellar Soul by David Rousseau
I am a stellar soul from the Great Central Sun experiencing earth through this human avatar.
1. Extraterrestrials   2. Aliens   3. Abduction
I. Rousseau, David – 1973-   II. Extraterrestrials   III. Title
Library of Congress Catalog Card Number: 2023942269
ISBN: 9781956945720

Cover Design: Victoria Cooper Art & Davian Art
English Translation: Nadège Tissot
Book Set in: Alexandar Quill and Times New Roman
Book Design: Summer Garr

OZARK
MOUNTAIN
PUBLISHING

PO Box 754
Huntsville, AR 72740
800-935-0045 or 479-738-2348 fax: 479-738-2448
www.ozarkmt.com
Printed in the United States of America

Contents

Contents

Preface

When David asked me to write a preface for his book *Beyond Our World*, I first declined his offer. But then I thought it was an opportunity to explain what the Be Light Editions Association is.

It was born from my desire to share some books I had read or translated with other people interested in these topics. At first, I published the books I had already translated, which enabled me to learn much about this new job.

As readers discovered B.L.E. books through word of mouth and a little help here and there, some authors, who identified with the values we defend, came knocking at our door to be published by Be Light Editions.

I must admit that my choices are quite subjective. I let myself be guided intuitively, just as I do for the books I translate, and I thank my guides for their precious help in this area. They always guide me toward the next book, the next author.

This is how I met David, first through emails, then through his help in the making of a book cover, and eventually with a physical encounter during a book fair.

I immediately felt it was obvious. What he was telling me was a synthesis of diverse topics related to what I call "our invisible team," a team not invisible to David, since he can see them!

So here is the first book of the series, which will include four volumes. I am very proud to present it to you. This story, which could be described as fabulous, incredible, or extraordinary, is not. It is even better indeed: it is real.

David's story met the criteria on which I chose the other books I have published: the sincerity, the author's desire to share warning messages that always stay positive, and above all, true love from our brothers in space, from these extraterrestrial civilizations that want to help us.

In his story, I have found many elements I already know, which were evoked in Dolores Cannon's books or in the testimonies of other abductees like Michel Desmarquet in *Thiaoouba, the Golden Planet* and Stefan Denaerde in *UFO Encounter from Planet Iarga*.

The book will not leave you unmoved either. The "plot" is supported by a dynamic, smooth style and a fast pace, which, I have no doubt, will make it impossible for you to put the book down after starting it, even if you only consider the story an entertaining piece of fiction.

To those of you who are in doubt, I would mention what Michel Desmarquet liked to say in the prologue to his book: "it's not enough to believe, you have to know." And just like him, I would also recommend reading the book several times to memorize all these precious teachings, because that is first and foremost what it is about.

And I will close by saying that the book is also a challenge for you, because if ignorance protects you, knowing compels you to question your belief system, to accept the link there is between the different so-called conspiracy theories, which are often handled separately, and to understand that WE ARE ALL INTERCONNECTED AND BROTHERS.

—Malou Panchèvre

Acknowledgments

First and foremost, I would like to humbly thank the Source with my deepest appreciation, gratitude, and unconditional and eternal love.

I express my deep affection for my "galactic family" and their loving and wise presence, and in particular Ezahyel, Pte San Win, Zarhya, and Kalhynda.

To my "earthly" parents, who have always loved and supported me since I was born, you have my eternal love.

I also want to extend thanks to the one who has become my partner as well as my Twin Flame. Thank you for your love, your presence, your unwavering support, and the trust you have put in me through this life experience.

Thank you to Isovah and family for what and who you are. To my sister, my brother, and their respective families.

To Morgan and his family, Stan and Nathalie, Marie-Noëlle and her family. A special thank you to Malou and Be Light Editions.

Thanks also to those who have shared moments of my life and have gone their own way.

And finally, I thank all those who have, in one way or another, helped me with the making of this book.

With love.

We are one.

Mitakuye oyasin.

—David, November 1, 2019

Foreword

What you are about to read in this book will probably seem incredible to you. I am not asking you to believe. Only to open your mind and your heart to other possibilities. I have kept many things to myself since I was six, and I have done so to this day. These are my personal experiences, my journey through life and my evolution, both human and spiritual, and even galactic.

I have shared much of my life experience with family, friends, and other people I have since lost touch with, but I have never before revealed it all. That is why I have decided to put pen to paper and tell you my story. I have always been an "experiencer" of the soul, a craftsman of life, a messenger, and an intuitive artist. Between 2000 and 2010, I became my own boss and set up an online Native American arts and crafts shop, while becoming a singer, a musician, and a composer in parallel with this activity. I just loved singing. It felt so good. I even created a duo with someone who was passionate about Native American culture and who was to become one of my best friends—a brother. We performed in themed restaurants and world music festivals. The duo soon became a band, and it all worked fairly well. We started to make a name for ourselves.

Gigs, in-studio collaborations with other artists, video shootings, etc. I believed in it and put all my energy into the band. The members that joined my band were mostly friends and I even considered them as brothers. But for some of them, the ego, the mind, and their personal interests took over. I am not blaming anyone, mind you. Things being what they should be in the moment, everything was perfect. Yet this was the calm before the storm. I am not going to say more on the matter. The fact is that I distanced myself and the group was disbanded.

Even if it is still hard to comprehend nowadays for some people, I have never been self-interested. I have always been into sharing and exchanging without expecting anything in return. They may not have been able to see it, but I hold no grudge, far from it. I forgave them long ago. Some people come and go in our lives. We share our life journeys and experiences for a longer or shorter period of time. Here lies the beauty of the moment.

We should not get stuck in the past and in bad memories. We should always move forward, not stand still and stagnate. For life is movement. Life is change. When everything changes, change everything!

All I remember from this time is that in 2006, I was appointed Ambassador for Universal Peace for some song lyrics I had written and performed on stage, and also that I had some amazing encounters with artists from the four corners of the globe: Mongolia, Siberia, Australia, Africa, the United States (Native Americans), Tibet, etc.

I give thanks again to all these true human beings for the magnificent exchanges we had.

Through my observations and experiences, I have gained quite a wide understanding of consciousness and, above all, I know who I truly am.

Creative thinking, intuition, inspiration, imagination, and joy are my main tools. Exploring, embodying, and living Who I Truly Am are my reasons for being in this life (and all others).

We are experiencing great changes on Earth and in the universe.

As human beings, we are currently going through a difficult time, where the meaning of life gets lost in the twists and turns and the cogs of modern society, which tries to crush us a little more every day through power, money, materialism, rules, laws, very tenacious false beliefs, and new technologies.

If we are not careful, this digital age is going to take us away for good from our true nature and as a consequence, from who we really are. The *Terminator* movies show this quite well. In an increasingly connected world, artificial intelligence prevails over man and turns against him. I do not want to sound alarmist, but this is one of the infinite possibilities we have to consider. On the spiritual level, by contrast—and this is the paradox—the universe is full of them—we are experiencing a magnificent transition period.

This transition is really important, because it will enable us to move from a three-dimensional to a five-dimensional world.

That is, all the illusions will fall away, one after the other, as humans become aware of their true place in the universe and of who they really are, so they can move out of duality and into love at last.

More and more of us are feeling and experiencing these changes—present and to come—which transform our mindsets and our consciousness and which affect all aspects of our lives and of life in general as we have always perceived it and lived it until now.

Life is going to be deeply "shaken up." And it has already begun.

In other worlds, the old patterns, the old ways of thinking and seeing things, of feeling, behaving, and living our lives are about to disappear (or fade) to give way to change and renewal.

But what are these significant changes?

We have reached the end of this journey in the third dimension to move into a higher consciousness, from the fourth dimension (which is the transition I mentioned earlier) to the fifth.

What is this passage through dimensions? What does it consist of? What impact will it have on us? On life itself? On the Earth?

We are actually all multidimensional beings, even if you are not fully aware of it yet, because our true being, our essence, what we really are, is a soul.

Our soul goes through time-space—and unlike what we are made to believe, it is not time that passes by—to have many experiences we call LIVES and/or INCARNATIONS, not only on Earth, but also elsewhere in our universe and far beyond, and this in different dimensions or densities, so the soul remembers what it really is and lives it to the full.

Why are these changes occurring now? In actual fact, they started a long time ago. Several millennia ago, according to my "star brothers and sisters." There have indeed been what I call these "energy waves" stretching out from the heart of the cosmos—the Great Central Sun—and spreading across the galaxies, just like waves which spread and expand on water when you skip stones.

These waves are quite powerful and their "effects" have been minimized by highly evolved beings—whom I call the star nations or star brothers—to "protect/prepare" us, as humankind was not yet awake enough for this mutation or transformation.

Our planet has somehow been quarantined and is surrounded by a huge magnetic grid acting as a filter to reduce the magnitude of these energy waves—the grid was also set up for other reasons that I will come back to later—and thus, to give a little more "time" to humankind to become aware of things. This energy spreads everywhere in the cosmos in order to enable the evolution of the world or worlds it touches. But let's stop here for now. We will have the opportunity to elaborate on these topics later.

I invite you now to discover my story and to go on this journey with me ... a journey which goes far Beyond Our World.

Introduction

Far, Far Away in the Galaxy

"Now, Kie'Teir, are you sure you want to incarnate with an avatar in this life sphere that Planet Earth is?"

"Definitely. It is a choice I thought through."

"Are you aware of the hardships you will have to face?"

"I have never experienced anything like this on such a life sphere before, so I don't really know what these concepts of 'separation,' 'fear,' 'suffering,' 'unease,' or 'solitude' really mean. In fact, the only thing that puzzles me, if I may say so, is 'death' ... I can't comprehend this idea of ceasing to exist forever. We know that it is impossible, yet human beings are convinced it is so. In any case, my soul wishes to 'go down' and experience all this, to bring my light to contribute in my own way to the change in consciousness."

"When you are there, limited by the envelope of this avatar and wondering what you are doing in this place, you will understand ... From this state of consciousness in which you have always been until now, you cannot even guess what it means to experience density and limitation."

"I'll take up the challenge ... My choice is made."

"So, if this is your will, I can only wish you a safe journey into the three-dimensional world and 'remind' you that we will be by your side watching and guiding you from this dimension. If you can open your heart wide enough—a task which is not easy at all, as you will see—you will be able 'to listen to us' and perceive our presence."

"And what is the best way to open the heart?"

"Observe everything that is going on inside. Listen to your inner voice. Take it easy and let go of the resistance to the fact that things on Earth are not as you wish. Accept yourself as you are. Only then can you accept others and honor their experiences. The peace and love which will arise in you as a result of this acceptance will automatically put you 'in touch' with us."

"All right, I will keep it in mind."

"No, son … You will forget it. These are the 'rules.' You will have to remember this when your physical body is already contaminated by judgments, attachments, and negative beliefs and is growing into adulthood. The light of your soul must emerge amid the darkness of fear, mistrust, and misunderstanding. Have faith, our beloved. We are certain you will manage. For you actually already have."

From my father's left hand emerged a holographic projection with three spheres.

"What's this?"

"It is the womb of your human mother. And this little embryo you can see inside is the avatar you will incarnate with."

"Yes, everything is planned. I have agreed with the soul who will travel with this body … She will 'make way' for me when she reaches the age of six Earth years."

"Have a good trip, stellar soul! Have a good trip, son!"

"Good-bye, Father!"

"The love of Source is with you. We love you."

CHAPTER 1

The Reminder

It happened in August, in the summer of 1981. I will forever remember that period of time, because several extraordinary events would occur in my life.

I had just turned eight in April and I had already been reflecting on some important issues for about two years, despite my young age.

"Why don't I feel I belong on Earth? Who am I? Where do I come from?"

I had that very deep, nagging feeling inside since I was five or six years old. I did not feel at home. I do not mean only here in France, but especially on this planet. It was both strange and unsettling. I felt like a foreigner, uprooted from his country, from his origins, but without knowing what they were. As if you knew you had lost your memory and yet the answers were there but were inaccessible. I could feel it in all my being, but I could not pinpoint it.

I was enjoying the beautiful summer day, playing outside with my friends in the small park located at the back of the building where I live with my family in Nantes, in the Loire-Atlantique French department. In the garden, we used to draw large circuits on the ground for the races of our toy cars, which we propelled with our marbles. It was awesome for me. I will always have fond memories of those times. The central area was made up of fine grey earth and was surrounded by trees and other buildings. It left an incredible opening to the sky in the center. These details are important, and you will understand why later on. Still, I loved the place and spent a lot of time there.

I did not have an unhappy childhood, quite the opposite. Despite their modest income, I think my parents did all they

1

could to make sure their children did not lack anything. As far as I can remember, we were fairly free to do what we wanted and to live our lives as children. I have no memory of prohibitions or obligations.

My parents have all my gratitude for this. The love and freedom we had enabled us to fully express who we were. I was very often amazed at a variety of things: nature and its beauty, the sky and its countless stars, the new cartoons coming straight from Japan—mangas—and Japanese cartoon movies that were making a dramatic entrance in France at the time, as well as toys and especially figurines. I was also very passionate about drawing and I have worn many pencils to this day.

Now, let's go back to that famous day in August. I had just come back to our flat to shower and have dinner with my parents, my sister, and my brother. At the end of the meal, I told them I wanted to go back outside to play. They agreed and asked me to come home before dark; it was the summer holiday, which means we could spend more time outdoors. I agreed too. So, I went out again, delighted and smiling from ear to ear. When I arrived at the park, I took my figurines out of my bag and started to imagine a whole world. I was not, I must say, lacking in imagination or inspiration.

I invented adventures for my beloved plastic characters, each more extraordinary than the last.

Then, I suddenly realized that the night was falling. It was already almost dark. I had not seen the time go by. Quite normal for a kid playing passionately, you might say. Except I had the strange feeling that time had been altered or even accelerated.

I looked up to the sky. It was magnificent. There seemed to be millions of stars. The show was impressive. I was fascinated by such beauty and vastness, which rose up around us, and at the same time, it looked so familiar. I could not explain it to myself, but I felt quite a powerful connection to the stars. I was more and more convinced, deep inside, that I did not belong to this world. It seemed self-evident, certain.

The questions I had been reflecting upon resurfaced in my mind and a stream of thoughts invaded me, mixed with a kind of melancholy. As if I had left my family there, or my loved ones.

"I want to go home," I said to myself.

I was still gazing at the stars and I started talking to them. I thought out loud, without any hesitation: "Listen to me! If you are really there, please give me a sign!"

To tell the truth, I did not really know who I was addressing my request to, but I realized I was giving more and more strength to these words. It came from my heart and I could feel it beat harder and harder in my chest.

"I beg you, if you hear me, show me that you can hear me and that you are there! And so I spoke!"

I did not know where those last words had come from. I no longer understood. They had given me shivers, not out of fear but rather as if I had known them for a long time. Another mystery to be added to my list.

A few moments after I had gotten lost in my thoughts, I saw an intense bluish-white light appear in the sky, to my great surprise. It was moving and becoming bigger and bigger.

I was amazed and excited and went on watching it without losing sight of it. It moved closer and closer. In an instant, the strange bright shape was above me and stood there, completely still. It was staggering.

I could figure out a round shape inside the light, but I could not make out anything else, because the brightness was getting more intense. There was no sound … but a kind of vibration and electricity in the air.

Then in a flash, the object disappeared. There was nothing left. It took me a couple of minutes to come to my senses. I then slowly looked down and there, to my great astonishment, I saw him before me.

He was standing up straight with a deep, gentle gaze. A smile spread over his lips. He had long straight black hair. His skin was bluish and shimmered slightly.

This being was peering at me, yet I felt no fear. Quite the opposite. I was delighted to see him and confident. A strange feeling suddenly came over me. It was as if I knew him. There was a kinship I could not yet explain.

My body seemed to stand still and vibrate with every cell when I realized this.

"David, I am delighted to see you (again). Don't worry, I will answer your questions."

What was going on? How was it possible? He was talking to me, but without words coming out of his mouth, as I did not see his lips move.

"You asked to see us and we heard you. I am here. You have many questions, and I will answer some of them."

At that moment, I received pictures, words, and sounds in my head or thoughts or mind, I don't really know. In any case, it was intense. Tears streamed down my cheeks.

He then told me: "And remember these words well, David: Mitakuye oyasin. You will understand what they mean later, because in actual fact, you know them already. You will just have to remember them. Good-bye, and see you soon, David. We love you."

Our Choices

Life is truly wonderful. We generally think it is just a series of random events and that the course of our lives is turned upside down by a simple throw of the dice. But there is no such thing as chance. There are only synchronicities.

And through these synchronicities, there are always moments where "fate" confronts us to this higher dimension of our being, through which our truth is revealed.

From then on, the illusion of chaos suddenly takes on the shape of a carefully orchestrated system, similar to a meticulously tuned clock. The workings of that celestial mechanism remain hidden from our senses and our understanding until their action becomes insistently manifest in our reality and our daily lives.

Subconsciously, each of us keeps on following a predetermined path. Our souls have chosen these paths before we "incarnated." There is a main road, a guideline which is intersected by multiple crossings and, depending on the choices we make and our decisions, infinite possibilities are offered to us according to the path we precisely decide to take.

And "signs" or "beacons" mark out our lives. But there you go, most of us refuse to take them into consideration because what we want above all is to preserve our patterns and illusions and to stay in our comfort zones.

Thus, we willingly lock ourselves within the walls of reason which, instead of liberating our freedom-thirsty minds, has the reverse effect of keeping us imprisoned in appearances.

The vast majority of human beings perceive their three-dimensional experience primarily through the left hemisphere of the brain, which is the seat of the rational mind—but again, this is from the rational, scientific perspective because in reality, our spirit inhabits each and every cell in our bodies.

When they came and took part in this fabulous life experience, they were disconnected from about 90 percent of their brain capacity, as well as from many of their body's energy systems, so they could live this experience in a three-dimensional world ruled by duality.

Each human being has actually received an implant of non-earthly origin by negative entities in order to block their personal and spiritual evolution. (I will discuss this more thoroughly in Book 2.)

This is why most human beings operate with only around 10 percent of their true capacities. The rational mind's development serves humans well in that specific context and environment. Its sole purpose is to protect them and help them fit in. Yet because of the fear that dominates it and the misuse humans make of it, the rational mind perceives life more in terms of limitations than in terms of the infinite possibilities and the multiple opportunities that life really offers it—again, this is due to that famous alien implant.

Man has also imposed on the rational mind to perform all kinds of tasks for which it was not designed. As a result, man has come to depend on it far more than necessary, and to such an extent that the intuitive and creative right brain has become almost atrophied from underuse.

To be free is to be fully oneself. Truly, in every sense of the word.

But who are we really?

Many of us, if not the vast majority, still wonder. And many do not get the answers. I do not claim that I have insider knowledge, yet I can tell you that our true nature, our authentic being, is a soul.

Let me say it again: I will indeed repeat some things here, because circling over and returning to certain topics, key elements, is useful: we are souls, multidimensional beings, who experience and express what they are through their lives and their unique natures.

Who are we really as souls? And where do we come from?

Take the one we call God, Source, the creator, Allah, Wakan Tanka—The Great Mystery in Lakota, whatever its name, and understand that he/she is all and at the center of all things. The Source, wishing to live many experiences and to know itself in all its forms, decided to "part" with some aspects of itself. This is how countless small parts of it broke away and flew in all directions to spread across the cosmos and galaxies. These little parts of God were thus named souls.

And each one of these souls made a choice to live what it is in multiple worlds and dimensions.

Thus was the universe seeded, as I like to say.

Some souls chose their experiences in higher dimensions to stay close to their true state of being and therefore, express what they are to the fullest. Others chose to live in "lower" dimensions in order to consciously "forget" who they are for the sole purpose of "remembering" who they are.

It may sound unlikely, yet it is the reality. So, through this process, the Creator/Source instantly lives innumerable experiences through us, since we are originally parts of him/her.

The microcosm within the macrocosm.

Isn't it said that what is inside of us is oddly similar to the solar system and the stars? We are an integral part of this Great Whole contained in the Source.

Now, if God really exists, why has no one ever seen him/her?

I will try to answer this question as clearly and straightforwardly as possible. In reality, you see God without being really aware of it. Let me explain. Imagine a giant telescope capable of magnifying particles floating in space yet invisible to the naked eye. Well, that is not enough. Imagine a telescope that is even larger, then one that is even larger, and you will then observe there is a whole world, a system which was undetectable so far. You will then notice that every planet, every universe, every galaxy is linked by a network, like tissues somehow, that are not organic but energetic, and you will see that there is space between each celestial body. You can then understand that this space is not empty. It is much the same with our organs inside our bodies.

If you look up closely, there is space between each of them, but they are still linked and interconnected by tissues called fascia, by blood flows, etc. All this works like a network. Well, it is the same with the Source, if I may say so. And it really does contain everything. It is so "big" we literally cannot see it, quite simply because we only see the spaces between each body.

Do you understand? It is beyond our human understanding, to be sure, but it reflects what he/she has shown me and what I have seen. This is the best way I have found to explain things to you. As I write these lines, by the way, he/she is delighted to see me detailing this to you. I am not afraid to tell you that I can talk to him/her and he/she can talk to me. I am not alone in this, fortunately. Others can. I have known and met some of them. And surprisingly, all of you can as well. Yes, you can! As I told you before, there are many things I have kept to myself and I will give you more details as my story unfolds. Or not! No, I'm just kidding. A touch of humor does no harm, quite the opposite.

And to be honest, I don't really have a plan for this book. I let myself be guided and inspired by my soul in the present moment, without thinking of tomorrow. My soul has always guided me where I needed to be. I have been listening to it from an early age. It is always so.

It was important for me to tell you all this before getting to the heart of the matter and sharing with you my experiences and my life. It will make sense for you too. At least I hope so …

The Call of the Unknown

As you may have gathered, it all started in my early childhood. I could see and hear "things." The adults always said that it was just imagination, that these "things" did not and could not exist. Well, I assure you that they did and that it was not my imagination. It was real. It still is. Even more so nowadays, I would say.

Seeing what we call spirits and other entities was quite natural for me. Conversely, I could not understand why no one else could see them.

But "they" had somehow warned me by telling me that for the time being, no one around me was ready to see and hear, and that I needed to keep this to myself, at least at first, in order to protect myself from judgments, criticisms and, above all, misunderstanding.

As you know, people are quick to pigeonhole and label others, even more so when it comes to things that are not supposed to exist. What is different and unknown is scary. I think it is a pity that it has come to this.

Take, for example, the First Peoples. Among the Native Americans, children are taught that this is all real, that we have a connection to the Earth and to everything around us, visible and invisible. So, among these so-called primitive tribes, the way of life is based on the respect and love of all beings and all things, because human beings are connected to all that is. Native Americans have always been aware of this.

That is the opposite of Western man, who has strayed from this path and as a result, has cut himself off from the essentials.

So, are you ready to follow this path to the unknown? If not, perhaps you should stop reading this story now, because it is similar to those one-way streets on which it is impossible to turn back once you have driven into them. For those of you who wish to continue with me, I have to tell you the facts as they happened.

And I have much to say. I have had so many experiences—one of them of great importance, God is my witness—that I will need several books to share this with you.

Still, the encounter with this star being would alter the course of my life and change it forever in every aspect. Although he gave me many answers, for which I am still grateful, I had many more questions. What reassured me was that I now knew why I was there, although I did not quite know where exactly I came from and for what purpose. Since that event, four years went by without anything else happening (or so I thought at the time—many things actually happened), except of course the fact that I had grown and understood certain things. My human and spiritual evolution was just beginning.

So, it was the year 1985. A few months earlier, my parents had told us that we would be moving, as they were having their house built in a town north of Nantes, some twenty miles away.

I have to say that the news had deeply upset me. I was about to leave a place I loved, my best friends and, in particular, the place where I had my famous encounter. I felt something like a break in me.

CHAPTER 1

I am not scared of change, on the contrary. Every change is good, even though it sometimes does not seem so when we experience it. Yet I have to admit that I did not understand it at the time. What would happen once we were there? What would become of my friends? And did they know about it, up there? Would they be able to find me? I kept my cool and remained confident despite it all.

I didn't really have time to say good-bye to each and every one. My two best friends had moved away too. Life is movement. Life is change.

We arrived in our new home in the middle of winter, in January. The cold weather had set in and the building work was behind schedule. The work was not finished. The shutters were not set up yet as the facades and the finishing touches had not been done. We were cold at night, but there was nothing unbearable.

So, our new life began. The more time went by, the more I refocused on myself. It was a little like meditating, except that I did it in full consciousness, all the time, with exponential frequency.

I felt absolute well-being. I was increasingly calm, peaceful, and in harmony, both with myself and with what was around me. I had found paradise. No more noise or interference to disturb this balance, because the mind was quiet.

Without really realizing it at the time, I rose spiritually. I walked the recall trail and came out of that sleep phase to fully walk the road back to my authentic self. I got closer and closer each time to Who I Really Was ... I could feel it.

I went to the local primary school for the remaining months. During that time, I didn't really make any friends, just mates I would not see again, because I would go to secondary school in September. I did not really care, actually.

From then on, I took a step back and detached myself from everything.

The summer holiday came around. I took the opportunity to stay outdoors as often as possible. I must say that our town is full of places along the Erdre River that are each more beautiful than the next. All places filled with plenitude. The ideal place to recharge your batteries. And I felt this "need" to (re)connect with nature, to the earth, to water, to the wind even more ... without really knowing why.

One evening in August, something amazing happened again. I was playing outside as usual and enjoying the mildness of the night. All of a sudden, I felt a tingling sensation on the back of my neck. There was some electricity in the air again. Someone was coming.

I looked up to the sky. I only had time to see a light shape go by, a little like a shooting star. Yet it was not a star, because it was rising very high and very fast instead of falling.

"Wow!" I said, surprised and delighted at the same time. I looked down. And there, as on the famous night in Nantes, a being was standing before me. But this time it was different. It had nothing to do with my first encounter.

This being was smaller. He was about the same height as me. He seemed to have no clothes on. His skin was dark grey. He had a large head, which was very bulky at the back. And his eyes were very large and dark. Deep black. Nothing was reflected in them.

But above all, I had a feeling of fear. Or rather, my mind was on the defensive. It was actually not the first time I had seen that kind of being.

"Don't worry. I am here to give you something. You have nothing to fear from me," he told me.

I could also hear him in my head, or my thoughts. Very unsettling. Something told me to be wary, yet at the same time I felt I could trust him.

He exuded a kind of aura by his presence, like an incredible strength despite his small size. Yet he looked so frail, at least in appearance. He was communicating with me without moving from where he was. I received a lot of information and pictures.

He was showing me his home world, which was in agony. They had used up all the resources of their star system, Zeta de Reticuli, and had left their planet. As a consequence, they traveled widely in the universe. I also learned that another group, which indirectly belonged to their species, had "abducted"[1] me on several occasions. They conducted scientific experiments, genetic cross-breeding, and cloning.

Those beings only think of themselves. They serve their own interests first and foremost and think only of their own survival. I

1   Abduction: in ufology, kidnapping of a person by aliens.

learned that those negative beings followed the orders of another race, who is far more powerful, domineering, belligerent, and violent.

So, I learned there were evolutionary and involutionary forces involving countless worlds outside our own. The being understood why I was wary of him, as I had unconsciously taken him for one of those who had abducted me. The memories resurfaced in me.

The four years during which I thought nothing had happened to me were in fact a memory screen implanted so I would not remember. They had taken me away many times during that period and "erased" my memory each time. I also heard that I had an implant at the bridge of my nose. They use it to find me but also to study me, take measures, record and analyze my behavior, etc. Anyway, he made me understand that I was still going to be taken away from time to time and that it was important nonetheless.

I would understand all this better later, he assured me. He told me it was now time for him to go. No sooner had I heard these last words than a very intense beam of light appeared. They both disappeared in a split second.

I went home to go to bed with many pictures in my head and many questions. I said nothing to my parents, who were watching television, and I dashed to my room, which I shared with my younger brother.

I couldn't sleep, as I was still excited by what had just happened to me. Then, after a long while, I had an epiphany of some kind.

For a number of years now, I often woke up in the middle of the night, paralyzed, unable to move even a little finger ... and I prayed. I prayed as hard as I could, because a dark mass floated above me and wanted to take my body, or to get inside ... in any case, I did not let it happen. Some nights, it lasted for hours.

What did this demon want from me? And why me? I was convinced that it was a demon. Yet it was nothing of the sort. It was a false memory, implanted in my mind by those greys who were taking me by force, so I would not remember them and what they did.

"But how do they do this? And why? To what end?" I wondered.

"Thanks to their technology. Their activities are beyond

human understanding. They create hybrids," a voice inside me suddenly told me.

"But who are you? Where do you come from?"

"Who I am does not matter. Yet, be sure of one thing, I am always here and I will always be. It cannot be otherwise. For now, you need to be patient. You will have all the answers in time. I am happy to meet you again, David."

"Happy to meet me again? But who exactly are you?"

I asked the question several times, to no avail. It was radio silence. What was going on? Was I going mad?

The voice was heard again: "Is a madman mad or are we all mad?"

I had to admit that he had a sense of humor. I had just read this sentence a few days before in a Batman comic. If I remember correctly, the Joker had asked the question to Batman.

"It was an image, a figure of speech. I am not mad. Besides, what is madness?"

"There is no such thing as madness!"

"Isn't there, now? What is it, then?"

"A concept, an idea, a hypothesis, a theory, a belief … maybe all these at the same time."

"Wow! Could it be that …?"

I did not have time to finish thinking.

"Yes, David. Man has long been in the habit of putting words to things he does not understand and which are therefore beyond his current skills concerning psychology and mind, physiology and emotions. He theorizes and when it fits his rational, scientific ideas, he names them and classifies them."

"That's incredible!" I exclaimed.

"In truth, it's nothing compared to the answers and information you will soon be getting."

"Getting? From whom? How? When? I've had enough! Will you tell me who you are in the end?"

"You have many questions, which I understand. But please be patient. Don't rush headlong like a ram"—another nice analogy as I am an Aries.

"Use the wisdom you have within you. All the answers to your questions are there, deep inside, in your cells, in your mind, and in your heart. Now you need to get some sleep. Your body needs it."

CHAPTER 1

It was late, between 1 and 1:30 a.m. I had completely lost track of time. I got up around 10 the next morning, feeling great. After all, it was the holiday. You can afford to sleep in late. What's more, I still thought about what was said overnight. I went to have my breakfast, both puzzled and reassured.

But whose voice was it? Who was he? And why did he speak to me? I wondered. I did not understand it all and yet, I was fairly confident, serene even.

I definitely had more questions than before. Who was going to give me the answers? Were there any answers to these questions anyway?

"Yes, there are, David," the voice resumed.

"Oh! You are still here," I shouted out.

"Yes. It will always be so. Remember what I told you last night. I am always present. I always will be."

"What's the matter? What's wrong?"

"What?"

That was my mother talking to me. She must have noticed I was lost in my thoughts and assumed I was in a daze. "No, I'm fine. I just had a bad night's sleep, that's all," I replied.

She did not mind. After breakfast, I got up and went to the bathroom to wash up. As I brushed my teeth, a silhouette appeared in the mirror in front of me. I was surprised and dropped my cup, which was full of water. I turned around to look behind me, but I was alone in the room.

What was it? Who was this? What was happening to me? And why was this happening to me? I definitely couldn't understand a thing anymore.

I went back to my room and lay down on my bed. A huge flow of thoughts then invaded me. For at least half an hour, it was a profusion of thoughts. Then without me explaining it, I found peace and quiet. Absolute silence. It was as if my body had disregarded everything around it. I felt lighter and lighter. So much so that after a while, which I could not measure time-wise, I found myself floating to the ceiling above my body.

It was unbelievable. And what a strange feeling it was at the same time to see myself down below.

"Am I dead yet?"

"Hahaha … not, not at all! Your experience here on Earth is far from over. You have all the time you need for your mission," a voice told me out of the blue.

"Who are you? And where are you?"

"Right here, David."

I spun around. I could have sworn he was behind me. Very close, even.

"Are you playing hide and seek?"

"No, not at all. We can play if you want. But as things are, I have a huge advantage, don't you think?"

"Of course, you do! You're invisible!"

"Invisible! Not really! Let's say it is a question of perspective and perception. It will be up to you to adjust your vision and frequency if you want to be able to see me."

"But how? What do I have to do?"

"The work is already underway, David. And the progress you have made lately is just perfect in the moment. Don't rush it. Everything happens or is realized at a given moment. Trust yourself. And trust us."

All of a sudden, I was in my body again. In my room. There, lying on my bed. I still felt the floating feeling and I had a little trouble coming back to reality. To this reality.

It was wonderful. One feels such a sense of well-being, to the point that there are no words to describe it. Or at least, I can't find any.

When I opened my eyes again, I realized everything was different. It was unbelievable. All I saw through my bedroom window radiated energy. I could see sparkling droplets floating or twirling, not only all around me but also outside. I went out to find out for sure.

It was everywhere. Even in the sky. How could I have missed this? It was not there before. It couldn't be.

"Of course, it was there. You just couldn't see it before."

"What do you mean?"

"David, you are awakening and evolving spiritually. Your perceptions and feelings are increasing. Your vision is adjusting and expanding further into other frequencies and perspectives. Your visual field is widening. In other words, you are activating your third eye."

"My third eye?"

"Precisely. It corresponds to the sixth chakra. What some of you call the inner eye, or the soul's eye."

"That's great! So, that's why I can see these drops of energy floating everywhere?"

"Yes. These drops, as you call them, are simply the flow of energy, which is everywhere and in all things. It is the energy of life spreading throughout everything. Without it, there would only be the void. And through this energy, we are all connected and interrelated."

"Wow! I'm starting to understand and to ..."

"No, you are starting to remember, David."

"Remember?"

"Yes, indeed. The shape and appearance you have today are not who you really are. Your body is only a vehicle for you to move through this world and this reality. Your body is not you. Let's say it is an expansion of your true nature."

"In that case ... er, what am I? Where do I come from?"

"You will have to find the answer to this question within yourself. Or rather, you will have to remember. Know this, however: You come from very far, far away. Not from a place on Earth, no ... from a place beyond the stars. And this is the first experience you have come to live in this life sphere. This explains your feeling of not belonging to this world. And you are right. For in your heart is the truth, your truth.

"The more you are centered in yourself and in your heart, the more you will understand, see, and live things."

"Thanks a lot for all this. May I ask you another question?"

"Yes, of course. Please ask."

"Who are you?"

"I knew you were going to ask me the question again. Let's say that all you have to know now is that I am your friend. Your best friend. And even more than that. What matters most here and now is that you remember. Remember who you really are in order to accomplish the task for which you came. You have come in a specific space-time period, because there are many changes to come on this planet. This choice you have made, this decision you have taken, are the greatest gift you could have given yourself. And it is wonderful."

"The greatest gift? I don't understand."

"Be patient. Please be patient, David. You will understand this over time. You will really grasp the meaning of all this. In the meantime, you now know that you are not alone and that you have never been, for that matter. There are just veils separating us. And one by one, you will drop them. What is the most important thing you have to remember right now, David?"

"To remain in the heart?"

"Exactly! You do listen. You really listen and that is a very good thing. You have always been a good listener, for as long as I can remember."

"If I understand correctly, we have known each other for a long time, haven't we?"

"You have no idea yet, but you could say that indeed. Let's say that time does not exist where I am. There is only the present moment. This will be explained to you later. It is much too early to tell you about the mechanics of the universe, about the matrix, and to reveal some of their secrets."

"Time does not exist?" I insisted.

"No, it doesn't. At least not the way you perceive and experience it. It is something that is quite malleable and not set. Nothing is set. Everything is in constant motion. Continuously."

"I don't get it all … I'm out of touch here …"

"Don't worry, you will understand this as you evolve. Not only will you understand, but you will remember."

"Will you always be here?"

"The answer is: will you always be here?"

"What do you mean? I don't understand."

"Will you always be listening? As you are now?"

"You mean, listening to you? To the spirits? To the star beings?"

"Listening to your heart, David. Listening to your authentic being."

"You mean it's all happening in my heart?"

"It is. To put it simply, let's say that it happens in the heart and through the heart. Now, you have to go home, your mother is expecting you for lunch. See you soon."

Lunch? Was I out that long talking to him? Where did the time go? It was really incredible, I felt like it lasted a quarter of an hour at the most.

Anyway, I found it all so exciting and magical that I went home starry-eyed. And with a billion questions in my mind …

CHAPTER 11

Illusion

It is essential for man and for his evolution to recognize and accept the existence of all aspects of the three-dimensionality in which he lives, so that he can understand them better.

The notion of time passing by, the duality and separation are intimately interwoven into the fabric of this 3D matrix—a matrix which is nothing but an illusion implemented by involuted entities. (I will come back to this later.)

If you try to understand only one aspect of it, the matrix will manifest with greater intensity to keep your attention and keep you within it.

As you become more conscious of the existence of this illusion and its repetitive patterns, you will then be presented with the choice to step out of the matrix. You can thus be reborn and remember who you really are.

You will be free to move again beyond the limitations of the third dimension. And so, you will realize that there are infinite possibilities offered by your higher self from the fifth dimension and far beyond.

In the third dimension, everything is molded, compartmentalized, and categorized. Take for instance unconditional love … It is not supposed to exist in the third dimension.

If you live in unconditional love, then you have reached the fifth-dimensional level of consciousness. And it means that you were able to step out of the illusion. It will be easier for you to understand the whys and the wherefores. For others, it will be harder to realize who is pulling the strings behind the scenes. It will only happen if you stop seeing the world as it is in its illusion.

To do so, you absolutely need to refocus. By placing yourself

17

in the heart, you will understand that we are all one, for we are all connected. You will understand that there is no separation because it is impossible to separate things.

When you are grounded to Mother Earth, you feel the love she has for us and you connect to the universe, to that Great Whole we are all part of. It cannot be otherwise because, once again, there is no separation.

Unfortunately, many people are still unable to escape and free themselves from the grip of the three-dimensional matrix. The third dimension offers no possibility to make conscious choices, in that everything is set and molded, right down to the way you think, act, and react.

You do not deliberately choose what you think, feel, and do at every moment of your life. In short, you are pushed to live in one way and not another: "Go to school. When you finish your studies, get a job. Get married. Have children. Pay your taxes. And obey the laws and regulations."

In other words, continue to be little sheep and follow the herd. Don't think for yourself. Don't feel things for yourself. Don't live in love because only money, fear, and control matter. If you let go of that, you will be free ... and, well, that is out of the question.

We are being kept in this system of illusions. Kept? But by whom? By what?

For now, I will leave these questions unanswered. It is important to understand things correctly and to put them into context. There is no point in rushing things. According to the turtles, as a Native saying goes, we shall "make haste slowly."

And remember that thought is creative. You create your own life through your thoughts. Creative thinking is the most powerful tool that we have been given. So pay attention to your thoughts.

Thoughts filled with tumult, stress, anger, frustration, etc., will influence your life and drag you down. Constructive, positive loving thoughts—toward yourself and others—will raise your vibration and your frequency. This is the power of creative thinking. Truly.

This is what some call "the Law of Attraction."

"Ask and you shall receive."

It is partly true. Except that we do not invent anything. Everything already exists. All we have to do is reach out and, depending on the form of our thoughts, whether they are constructive or destructive, we reap the rewards. Others call this karma. Yet, karma does not exist either. It only exists in your thoughts and the patterns set up in this 3D matrix.

To sum it up, change your ways of thinking. Don't let the mind, ego, or rational mind dominate you. Instead, place yourself in the heart. In this manner, you will free yourself from the chains of the matrix. You will awaken your intuitive capacities and free the creative power lying dormant in you. We are all Creators and co-creators.

Therefore, you have two options:

The first one is to endure the life created by that system and to remain prisoners of the illusion through these false beliefs and patterns, in slavery.

OR

The second option is to create your life in peace, harmony, and love.

It is as simple as that. You may well pray but if your prayers are not creative, the universe will answer: "You want this, that's fine" and yet, it won't work.

For the universe to really listen to you, you have to be intuitive and assertive in your request. For example, if you say: "Please, God, give me this or that," it will not work. And your prayers will not rise above the fourth dimension.

But if you make your request by stating things in the heart, the result will be quite different. Let us take for instance a young artist going into music and wishing to make a living from his passion. His creative request will be made to Source in this way: "Creator of all things, thank you for having brought me success in the realization of my musical project and its distribution to the media. Thank you from the depths of my heart. With all my gratitude and love."

You shouldn't be scared to assert what you want in your life. The universe will really listen to you. And it will echo what you are asking for because, remember, we do not invent anything. Everything already exists. We just have to remember that and to ask for what we have actually created and chosen ourselves, in the fifth dimension.

This is exactly what I did when I left my job to establish myself as an illustrator and above all, to make a living from my passion and to do something I enjoy, something I have chosen.

From the time I created this thought and asked for it to the time it became a reality in 3D, it took about a year.

Everything had to fall into place and the synchronicities had to come together to create the request in the third dimension. It always takes a shorter or longer period of time for things to take shape and come to life here.

On April 5, 2019, I gave an interview[2] to Nicolas from the eveilhomme.com website, during which he asked me the following question: "You're self-employed. How did you know it was the right time to make a living from your work?"

"I am indeed! I set up my business just over a year ago now, after I left my job. I knew it was the right time because everything was falling into place. By that, I mean that the synchronicities were there. Thought is really creative, you know. I had wanted to make a living from my passion for a long time, so I created this action by thought so that it would come to life in our world, in our reality. Then, I was noticed by American Studios that shared some of my artworks. At the time, I wasn't called Davian art yet but David C Designs.

"I was even approached by the Promotheus Studio for one of my pictures. This is the studio that produces the Alien Theory show. Then, a writer asked me to draw his illustrations. I also started having requests from individuals for portraits of their guides or of a galactic family member. So, everything was falling into place. The road was laid out before me. I just had to follow it. That's how I knew it was the right time."

A New Life

I was now in sixth-form. I intentionally skip over my years at secondary school because nothing extraordinary happened during these years. Or at least nothing significant to burden you with; I continued going my own way in my spiritual evolution, as you can imagine.

---

2   The interview is available in French: https://eveilhomme. com/2019/04/05/davian-un-artiste-hors-norme-contactegalac-tique-écrivain.

I went to a vocational school in Nantes, because my parents unfortunately could not afford to send me to Fine Arts, the studies I had chosen.

I have to admit that at the start, I was reluctant to go and that the first year was tough for me. Not only was I unmotivated, but I was even less hard-working. My marks were going downhill, except in French, English, and drawing, where I was at the top of the class.

What was surprising, however, was that I saw people in that school that no one else could see ... at least not that I knew of.

On the one hand, it is insane to see how some negative entities get under the feet of some people and make them behave or react in certain ways. And on the other hand, there are these luminous entities watching over some others like guardian angels. This is a pretty good depiction of the notions of "good and evil" found in the scriptures and religions. But they are still far from the truth. Yes, I had learned, or at least remembered, that negative entities interact with us unbeknown to us.

It was also in that school I got to know those who would become my best friends. The first one was called Fabrice P. and he came to me the very first day saying: "Hi! My name's Fabrice. I hope we'll become good friends and we'll remain so!"

I will always remember that first day at school. I was both surprised and delighted, and I replied, "'Hi! Yes, I hope so too. I'm David."

In fact, there was a reconnection ... Our souls had recognized each other. We were soul brothers. But he was not aware of it. Or at least, he never told me. Still, a strong friendship/brotherhood was to ensue over the next four years.

Then, there was Franck V., with whom I would also have a strong friendship. Even if it's true that he acted a bit as if he were a big shot. He was tall and strong—six feet, three inches tall—and came from a disreputable neighborhood. But he was actually a big teddy bear.

I also met Christophe L., who was from the same town as me. We would become very good friends too.

Quite frankly, some totally unexpected events were to take place during those years at school.

In year 11, my mate Fab and I started talking of spiritism and ghosts. I don't remember how the topic came up. Still ... one day, in class—we were sitting at the back—we spoke to spirits through automatic writing. I even started making drawings transmitted from beyond. My friend was surprised by the accuracy. But gradually as we practiced, things started to happen.

First of all, words and sentences became more and more threatening ... and above all, I could see dark entities whispering things into the ears of some of the students. I told Fabrice about this and he understood my concern, but he still wanted to go on.

I may as well tell you that we were starting to play a little game that I would later dislike. It started with restless nights. More and more intense and disturbing nightmares agitated my mind. I was not scared, however. I knew that if I let the fear rise up in me, they would play on it.

Fab was excited despite the nightmarish nights he was also experiencing. Our experiments went on for months. One night as I was riding my moped back home, about twelve miles away, a dark shape suddenly appeared in the sky right in front of me, on a long straight road that led to my town. While not losing sight of the road, I looked at that strange apparition ... the more visible it got, the more it took on a somewhat devilish appearance.

I had about one mile to go to get home. The shape continued to change and grow to a size which I estimated to be around 98.5 feet. And then, I saw two horns on its head and volcanic red eyes ...

"I am the Devil," he said to me with a very gravelly voice. "From now on, you shall be scared! Very scared!"

"Yes, sure! Keep talking!" I replied.

He started laughing and threatening me further. All of a sudden, a horn sounded. I had veered away from my trajectory.

"Sorry!" I let out to the driver.

"You won't fool me in this little game. You want me to have an accident. This won't work. You know what, you don't even exist."

I repeated this—you do not exist—four times and he was gone. I must say that I had also prayed hard to God to protect me.

When I got home, I realized that we had gone too far. We mustn't fan the flames, so to speak. The next day, I would tell Fabrice I was done.

Decision

The next day, I left home earlier so I could see Fab sooner and talk to him. He was at boarding school all week, so I knew where to find him in the morning, before everyone else arrived. Once there, I found him where he liked to relax before starting class. He was sitting on a low wall at the back of the yard, facing the trees overlooking the middle of the yard, between the dining hall and the first building where the classrooms were.

"Hi, Fab! How are you? I need to talk to you," I said to him while shaking hands with him.

"I'm fine, thanks, and you? What's going on?"

I told him what I had experienced the night before. He could not believe it. I also decided to tell him what I knew about the negative and involutive entities and what they were capable of, without going into details because we were running out of time. He was shaken when I explained that these entities actually came from another world and that they controlled humanity through religions, dogmas, beliefs, society, power, and money.

In the end, he decided to stop playing and quit the game. And it was so much the better! It is always wise to listen to your heart and not to your mind, which those beings infiltrate. For their hold would be greater each time, should we fail to react.

In any case, I do not know whether he believed me, or whether he was scared, but he did not talk to me about spiritism afterward. Another topic had piqued his curiosity: UFOs. He wanted to know more. I shared everything I could tell him. I couldn't just throw everything at him out of the blue, even if he was my best friend.

UFOs

Fabrice quickly understood that UFOs were my pet subject. So, he wanted to know much more about them. But I could not tell him everything … Some things are better left unsaid if the person in front of you is not ready. There is no point in insisting … otherwise, it is a lost cause. And I knew that Fabrice was not ready to hear everything … far from it. My feelings have never misled me on these facts. I can understand that for some, it can be frustrating, but it is better that way.

I explained to him that not only was it my favorite subject but I also carried out some research from time to time and I investigated UFO sightings in the area. I was starting to receive more and more testimonies by mail. We did not have the Internet back then. We subscribed to periodicals like *Lumières dans la Nuit*,[3] which dealt with these so-called paranormal matters. We placed ads, we wrote short articles; only one of mine had been published, which kept us up to date with the latest cases listed.

Fab took a real interest in the topic and regularly asked me for information about what was going on. I told him there would soon be a meeting in Nantes's Petit Port, where some speakers, ufologists, would be present to talk about the UFO dossier. The conference would take place on a Wednesday afternoon. It was good timing because we never had classes on Wednesday afternoons. What a synchronicity. We set up an appointment.

I was both excited and wary. I did not really know why, but I could feel something strange.

"Well, it's no big deal. We'll see when we get there," I said to myself.

The Conference

The big day had come. We were sitting in the classroom and Fab asked me: "What is wrong? I feel you're distant ..."

"I'm fine. It's just that I've been feeling something about this meeting since the moment I told you about it."

"Feeling something? Can you explain?"

"To be honest, I can't quite nail it ... It's very vague ... but at the same time, it is like I'm being told not to go. I feel uncomfortable or something."

"Do you want to cancel?"

"No. I don't. I think we should go, even if it sounds paradoxical."

"OK! Good. With everything you've told me, I have to say

---

3   *Lumières dans la Nuit* is a French bimonthly ufology periodical set up by Raymond Veililith in 1958.

that I am a little confused."

"I'll give you that. But trust me, I haven't told you everything."

"What? What else is there?"

"We'll talk about it later. For now, let's go back to the lesson. The teacher has spotted us chatting."

"All right! But you'll tell me all I need to know."

"Deal," I replied.

On the whole, the morning went fairly quickly, but my confusion did not. It had even increased in intensity. Where did it come from? I just could not figure it out. It was as if something bad was about to happen. My senses were somehow on alert, like an animal suddenly feeling a terrible storm coming before it gets there.

Fab and I headed for the dining hall to have lunch. The fateful moment was fast approaching. After lunch, Fab took my bag to leave it in his room so I would not be burdened with it for the rest of the day. He joined me five minutes later and we left the school. We had to take the bus to get there.

The strange thing was that the place was quite close to where I used to live when I was a kid, and where I had that famous first encounter. Fab did not know about this part of my story. But I told him I had lived in that neighborhood as a kid.

We got there about twenty minutes later. We were early. Almost an hour early. We crossed the street to check the street number where the conference would take place. The bar, betting, and tobacco shop I knew was still there facing the racecourse. It looked so familiar to me, it was as if nothing had changed. It seemed so close in time. We walked past the tobacco shop and we saw that the conference was actually going to be at someone's home, as there was a small house squeezed between the buildings.

That's what I thought. I had no memory of a hall hosting such events. Fab told me that he suddenly felt nervous.

As we still had some time to spare, I decided to show him the place where I had lived.

"It's not far. It's five or six hundred yards from here," I said to him.

"OK! It will do me good to walk a little …"

While showing him around, I told him about my childhood, my friends, the long summer evenings I spent outside playing. He was happy to hear my story and what I had experienced. But I did not tell him the whole thing. It was not the right time yet.

"We have to get going. We're going to be late," Fabrice told me as he looked at his watch.

Men in Black

"Wow! I lost track of time," I replied.

"We're going to be a bit late now."

"That's OK. They need time to get everyone in, so I figure they won't have started."

We got there and, indeed, there were still some people arriving.

As we were about to enter the front gate, we found ourselves face-to-face with two people dressed entirely in black, hat, dark glasses, and briefcases in hand. I discreetly motioned Fabrice to continue on our way and not to enter the meeting place, as if nothing had happened.

One of the two men in black lowered his glasses slightly when he reached us. His eyes were completely black, without irises, and his skin was very pale white. Once they had passed us, I surreptitiously turned around. As they crossed the threshold, they both looked at me. I felt a paralysis come over me and a voice sounded in my mind: "We know who you are!"

I told Fabrice to start running.

"But what's going on? Will you just explain?"

"Later! Better not to stick around."

"So what do we do then?"

"We take the bus again and we go to Versailles Island, if you want. It will be quieter there to have a chat."

Versailles Island was one of our favorite places. We often went there in spring and summer to relax, chat, etc. We headed for our favorite place, where we could sit down and, above all, stay away from prying ears.

Fab was lost in his thoughts and he looked baffled. We let a few minutes go by in silence. Then, after a while, he asked me: "So, tell me ... What happened? Who were these people?"

"To be honest, I don't really know who these people are ...

CHAPTER 11

They are called Men in Black because, as you saw for yourself, they are dressed in identical black suits and they often have a hat and black glasses on ..."

"Secret agents, or something like that?"

"You could say that, except ... hold on tight, they're not really human."

"What? What's this about?"

"Well, from what we know, they're hybrids, half-human, and half-alien."

"You've got to be kidding me? You can't be serious."

"I'm afraid I am. From what I know, they would have been designed by those we call the Greys from their DNA and human DNA ... Their mission would be to watch very closely everything having to do with UFOs, witnesses, photos, recordings. When it is too disruptive, they strongly intimidate people ... and even worse, they go so far as killing inconvenient witnesses or people who know too much. Did you notice the color of their skin?"

"Er ... no, not really. I must say I didn't really have time to pay attention ..."

"That's true. Anyway, you would have seen for yourself that there was something different about them. In general, they have very light, pale white skin, a bit like albinos, and their eyes have no irises—at least you can't see them because their corneas are completely black. Others say they have seen some of them with almost luminous purple eyes ...

"And most importantly, they communicate telepathically."

"And did they tell you anything earlier on?"

"They did. They told me they knew who I was. That's why I told you to run."

"It's bonkers ... You have to admit it's hard to imagine and hard to believe! We are in full sci-fi here ..."

After a minute or two of silence, he went on: "What did you get me into, David?"

"I did not get you into anything, Fab! Remember, you wanted to know more, and I asked you if you were ready ... Now, you are beginning to understand that the world is not as we are shown and above all, as they try to show it to us."

"Is it dangerous? I mean, if I go by what you are claiming, they can know everything and find us anywhere, is that right?"

"There's a risk indeed. These things aren't supposed to exist, let alone happen but, yes, it can be dangerous ... I'd understand if you were scared."

"No, it's not that I'm scared ... Well, I am, actually. It's just that all this goes against what I know, what we know ..."

"Yes, it does! And to be prepared, we need to accept it and not be afraid of the current and future changes ... because things change and nothing can stop that."

"But who are you? The more time goes by, the more I discover aspects of you ... it's disturbing ... I don't know what to think anymore."

"Don't worry, Fab. Remember the first day at school? You came up to me and said: 'I hope we'll become good friends.' That day, you listened to your heart or your intuition, whatever ... So have faith, keep faith in our friendship. I can't tell you who I am, though. I can't tell you anything, for now anyway. I'm sorry."

"Are you kidding me? Cut the crap and tell me!"

"No, sorry, Fab, I can't tell you more. Let's move on now."

He had to resign himself, but it was tough and we kept quiet the rest of the afternoon. I understood how he felt, it takes time to integrate, accept, and experience these things calmly.

CHAPTER 111

A New Encounter

We had just started our fourth and last year in secondary school. Fab and I were still friends, the kind of friends that are joined at the hip. The years had even strengthened our bonds and you could say we were like brothers. But as is well known, all good things must come to an end.

Fab had quit so-called paranormal cases but we still had common passions, such as music, movies, strolls in Nantes, girls … Life went on as usual.

Apart from this wonderful friendship, I spent more and more time with Christophe, who lived in the same town as me, but in the countryside, about three miles north and close to the Erdre River. We met on the bus driving us to school and we used to see each other there in the morning and evening.

On a Saturday, when I was at his place, I met his mother and his sister. His dad was not there because his parents were divorced. I was invited to spend the evening there and have dinner with them, which I gladly accepted.

Once the meal was over, Christophe's mum had to go and there were just the three of us. Chris started talking to me about spiritism and how he would like to have a séance. He asked me what I thought of it. After I warned him that it wasn't to be taken as a game and that I had had some experiences in the field, he ignored my warnings and started getting the table ready to start the séance.

We wrote all the letters of the alphabet on small pieces of paper, which we then put in a circle in the middle of the table. Two larger pieces of paper with the words "yes" and "no" were positioned to the right and to the left. To replace the traditional Ouija board, we took a glass and turned it upside down so we could each put a finger on it to make contact. The séance had hardly started than there were some reactions. The glass started shaking and moving quickly. I was not surprised but Chris's sister, E., started to tense up.

I wanted to wait before taking action and let Christophe call the tune and ask his questions. What I expected happened. I saw a dark shape appear behind Chris and he started getting irritated. As he was not getting the answers he expected, he started insulting the spirit …

"Calm down, Chris. Don't insult him. You don't know who you have …"

I didn't have time to finish my sentence. The glass rose above the table and was thrown against the fireplace. A few seconds later, a huge crash was heard above us, in the attic … as if a massive wardrobe had been pushed down. We headed up to the attic. There was a retractable ladder and a trapdoor to open to access it. Chris took the lead and went up there first with a torch.

Once up there, they were dumbfounded. Nothing had moved. Nothing had fallen down. At the same time, a shattering of glass was heard downstairs in the living room. We went down as quickly as possible to see what it was about. E. was less and less reassured. You could see the fear in her eyes.

When we got to the living room, it was clear that nothing had moved there either and that nothing had been broken. Apart from the glass, whose broken pieces littered the floor, we did not see anything else.

"So, do you want to keep playing, Chris?" I asked him.

"No, that'll be fine for tonight," he replied, puzzled and doubtful.

"You understand better now why you shouldn't consider it as a game, but rather as something serious?"

"Yes … and I don't want my mother to hear about it."

"Don't worry, I won't say a word."

E. remained quiet.

"Are you going to be all right?" her brother asked her.

"Yes … yes," she eventually replied softly. "I don't want us to do that again!"

Her voice was still a little shaky. I think she had the fright of a lifetime.

"Is he still there?" she asked me.

"No, he's gone."

"Are you sure?" Chris asked me.

"Yes, definitely."

"How do you know?"

"Let's say I 'made' him go."

"How did you do that?"

"I can't explain for now. There is still too much you don't know. And it's getting late, I need to go home."

"All right. Will you tell me more next time?"

"We'll see, Chris. See you soon!"

A Being from Elsewhere

It was a regular school day in the spring of 1992. For many of us, it was the end of secondary school in a few months' time. Fabrice was going to live his fourth and last year at boarding school. He was really starting to get fed up with it. And that is understandable, as he only went home on the weekends during that period. On the other hand, he did not want our friendship to end. Neither did I, I have to say. I already felt a little sad. Besides, he did not really live very far—about forty miles away—and we could always meet up again afterward.

Anyway, it was a beautiful, mild, and sunny day. We were all outside during the afternoon break. It was an opportunity to have a smoke, for those of us who smoked. We were allowed to smoke in this school, provided we did not leave cigarette butts on the ground.

Everyone was going about their business until I noticed the schoolyard was dead silent. Everything went quiet.

No one was talking and a crowd was gathering down the yard, near the school entrance. They all had their heads up.

"What's up?" Fab asked me.

Sensing something unusual, I replied: "Let's go and have a look, quick!"

We dashed toward the crowd, because from where we were, the trees were in the way and we couldn't see anything.

And then, BANG!

Above our heads, at a height of approximately twenty or

twenty-two feet, a man was floating in the sky. At least, he looked like a man, with a humanoid body like us. The likeness ended there. On watching him closely, what I could see first was that he had no flying apparatus, nor did he make any sound or noise.

He had a kind of one-piece close-fitting silvery suit. There he was hovering above us. Everyone was as if hypnotized or in a daze, and no one was saying a word.

It was unbelievable! There was complete silence, I couldn't even hear the birds chirping, nor even the cars going by in the street below.

Every now and then, he would gently turn his head right and left, as if he was looking for something. He still had not moved from where he was and he was still floating, with his arms more or less at his side. His face looked as if it were covered with a helmet or a mask … in any case, I could see it was larger, taller, and longer than a human head. Then, he turned slightly while floating a little toward me. He stopped moving and looked at me. I don't really know what happened then … He was communicating … He was sending me something telepathically, but I could not understand. Then, there was a flash of light in my eyes.

I felt different straightaway, still the same yet something had changed in my memory … I could feel it. It was as if I could access dormant knowledge and/or memories. But it was still too vague in my mind to put things in order.

I started clearing my head and realized he was turning away from us and was about to leave.

"What's this? What is he?" someone in the crowd asked, breaking the silence.

As I saw that everyone was captivated and that nobody was speaking, I said: "Isn't he an alien?"

Everybody turned toward me and they all remained quiet and stunned.

The being was going, still floating up in the air. We could now see his back. No device whatsoever was fastened to him. Still no sound either. And he disappeared out of our sight behind the surrounding buildings, heading northeast.

The next morning, nothing was as before at school. I had arrived earlier to see Fabrice before class. We had a good half hour. I told him I wished to go to the local newsagent's to comb through the newspapers. We were quite disappointed. Not a single newspaper reported what had happened the day before.

Fab didn't know what to think. Once we were out of the newsagent's, he asked me: "How is that possible? We were not the only ones who saw him. There were certainly many more ... and not only in the school ... So, how come there's not a single article about it?"

"Censorship! That's the only thing I see, Fab. They must have hushed the matter up."

"There's bound to be someone who mentioned it ... or reported it?"

"Not necessarily. I'm also convinced that many others were able to watch him, but people choose to keep quiet out of fear. Out of fear of ridicule or of looking like a fool ... or fear of reprisal for family or others. And I'm sure many didn't understand what it was about."

Blackout

"What about the notorious Men in Black? We didn't see them?"

"No, that's true. Maybe they didn't have time to react or intervene."

We were back at the school and the atmosphere was very quiet compared to earlier on. One of the school supervisors arrived at the same time.

Fab called out to him without hesitation.

"Hi! How are you? Tell me, can we talk about what happened yesterday, I ..."

He was interrupted before he could ask his question.

"Don't talk to me about that. No more talk about that. Nothing happened, all right?"

The supervisor looked very nervous, frightened even.

"What's wrong with him?"

"I don't really know, Fab. But I think we're about to find out."

Indeed, the atmosphere was strange. Many other students scowled at me and then looked away. I could feel their fear, mixed with misunderstanding and even disbelief.

One of our teachers arrived too. I decided to go to him.

"Good morning, sir. Tell me, may I ask you something?"

"Hello, boys. Yes, I'm listening."

"Do you know about yesterday? Maybe you saw him too ..."

"Let me stop you right there, David. Nothing happened yesterday. Nothing. Do you hear me?"

"What do you mean? You can't say that! We all saw him. What's going on?"

"All I can say—and this is just between us," he whispered, "is that we've been ordered by the head teacher not to talk about it, so the topic is closed. Do you understand? No one is to bring it up anymore."

"Er ... very well," I agreed.

"I'm counting on you," he said, as he headed for the offices.

"I don't intend to stop there," I told Fabrice.

"We're going to get into trouble ... Maybe it's better to avoid talking about it again," he suggested.

"Oh, no. I don't agree. I'm going to look into this on my own. This is not normal. Either they're scared because the head has been threatened, or they are scared to find out what it really is. I think it's both."

"Threatened? By whom? By the Men in Black?"

"Probably ..." I replied without going into details. "The fact is that they are setting up a kind of blackout."

"How can they hush up something like that? It's too big, even I have to admit it ... Are you sure it's not a top-secret project? A trial for a new technology? And they just wouldn't want it to get out ..."

"No, trust me, Fab. The being we saw yesterday wasn't human at all. He passed something on to me telepathically."

"What? What did he pass on to you?"

"Well, I can't really tell you for now ... It is still unclear. I think he awakened something in me."

"Wow! Do you realize that? You mean he came for you ..."

"I wouldn't say that ... Maybe he also communicated with someone else at the same time ..."

I did not know what else to tell him, in fact, because as incredible as it may seem, the being did come for me, to deliver a message to me. Whatever the place and time, when it is the right time, it just is ... Space-time is very different for them. However, he really had to make a huge effort to materialize in this reality. We live in a fairly dense 3D world and he has a higher, lighter vibration and frequency … How come he showed himself in this way for all to see?

I really had to find the answers to these questions. There had to be a purpose, a reason. Later during the day, something else occurred. It was getting really unbelievable.

We had gone back to class as if it were a regular day, if I may say. I heard no one speak of our visitor and during our afternoon break, while we were all outside, we could smell an unusual, undefinable smell … It even bothered a lot of people, who started to cough …

For my part, I didn't feel any discomfort, except for the smell.

"What smells like this?" Fabrice asked me.

"I don't know. But it's weird indeed. I wonder if it's not related to what you know."

"Related to what? I don't understand."

"Well, you know, yesterday … our visitor …"

"What are you talking about, David? I was at the infirmary all day yesterday. I wasn't well. We didn't even see each other."

"What? No, we were together and something incredible happened … don't you remember?"

"What incredible thing? I'm telling you, I was at the infirmary all day."

"But that's impossible! You're kidding me!"

"Stop it! What's going on with you? What the hell happened yesterday?"

"Well … no … you know what? Forget it."

I no longer understood. What did this mean? As I wanted to find out for sure, I went and saw a couple more guys in my class to ask them some questions.

They could not remember anything either. It was as if they had forgotten … or as if their memory had been erased.

It was the last straw. Was I the only one who remembered what had happened the day before? No, it was not possible … That was enough to blow a fuse. There had to be an explanation.

"Yes, there is, David."

I recognized the voice that started to sound in my mind.

"Oh! Very well! What is it, then? Because I don't understand a thing here!"

"Are you ready to hear it?"

"Of course I am!" I answered fiercely.

"It is linked to the scent you could smell outside. It's actually a gas. A gas that was spread deliberately and that covered the whole city."

"A gas? What kind of gas? Who spread it?"

"The kind of gas that is not natural, as you might expect. It was designed a long time ago by those whom you call the involutive entities."

"For what purpose?"

"Its primary aim was to keep you in a sleep system. And here I mean all the people on your planet."

"But what for?"

"To maintain control. To maintain their power, which they have established for several thousands of your years. They have used that gas to prevent you from awakening spiritually and from remembering who you really are. That way, they could dominate you and use you for their own interests."

"Wait a minute … You mean, the whole of humanity was a slave to those beings?"

"Not 'was' … It still is."

"What?"

"Yes, David, you understood me well. In fact, the world as you perceive it and in which you live is only an illusion. An artificial 3D matrix they have set up and that is their playground to satisfy their interests and needs."

"Wow! Wow … So if I understand correctly, you mean all this is false? Everything around us is false? And our …"

"No, I'm not saying that either. The system upon which your society is based is an illusion. That system is false, rigged … but human beings have been in that system for so long they are sure it is reality. Their reality. And they have made sure you were kept inside all this time, so that no one is aware of the deception. Some have managed to escape, though. But so few of them, I must say …

"That's why it is a crucial time for you, here and now.

"Things are changing, things are evolving."

"Wait, please tell me … You are saying that some have managed to escape? How? Who?"

"The first ones were those you call masters ... masters of wisdom ... ascended masters ... and a few others that are unknown or little known to you. Some Starseeds or people who awaken to their true selves, researchers in ufology and exobiology too, people who got a little too close to certain things and wanted to disclose them. Some lost their lives because of that ..."

"You're talking about Jesus, right? He's the first ascended master I'm thinking of."

"Yes, among others. There was Siddhartha, Moses, Mohammed, Laozi, and many others ..."

"And they crucified Jesus. Was it for that reason?"

"Concerning Yeshua (Jesus), it's a little more complex ... Let's say that he was aware of what could happen and of all the valid alternatives. His existence at that point in your history is a choice he made. A choice of pure love. And he certainly shook the pyramidal hierarchy of those who rule in the shadow. His message was strong, powerful, and universal, but embarrassing to some. Too embarrassing even, if I may say so. That's why they decided to take his life. But as you know, death is an illusion. They thought they had managed to eliminate him, except that he actually went somewhere else when he was buried and regenerated ... Then he reappeared. Hence the confusion. Everyone thought he was resurrected and back from the dead."

"Wow ... that's incredible ... but at the same time, it's as if I knew this. But tell me, where did he go to regenerate?"

"This is for you to remember because, as you pointed it out, you do know. I have to leave you now. Your classes are starting again. See you soon, David."

Ezahyel

"Wait! One more thing, please ... What's your name? After all this time, I still don't know your name. And don't tell me to remember it."

"Ezahyel."

Ezahyel. The name vibrated in me and it was as if my heart recognized it completely. Images and memories suddenly flashed through my mind and I was transported light years away. Now I knew why he had looked so familiar when I first saw him at the age of eight.

Ezahyel, his name was still sounding in my cells when I went back to class. I might as well say that during the remaining two periods, I had my head in the clouds. I was thinking about everything Ezahyel had just revealed to me. But there was still one crucial point to be clarified: Who was the being who had come floating in the air the other day? I would have to ask him. I was sure he knew who it was. I realized Fab was talking to me. I had really switched off ...

"Sorry, what were you saying?"

Then, school was out. That was all for the day.

Well, I had not heard a thing. How long had I been lost in thought? I don't even know what the teacher talked about ... Phew. What a day!

"See you tomorrow. Have a good evening!"

"Thanks, you too, Fab. See you tomorrow."

Once I got home, my mother told me she thought I looked tired.

"Yes, it's been a tough day," I replied. "I think I'm going to go to bed right after dinner."

Somehow, I wanted to tell her everything, but I couldn't. It was still too early. I went to my room and lay down on the bed. Too many thoughts were pestering me. I needed to meditate to refocus and see things more clearly.

The familiar tingling sensation soon came and after a couple of minutes, I saw a great bluish glimmer turn all around me. It was both beautiful and mysterious. I could not define what it was. When I stared at it, it moved away. When I reached out with my hand, it moved away again. But what a feeling of well-being, joy, and plenitude ... What was happening? Who was it?

Even though I could not distinguish any real shapes, it was definitely someone and he or she had such a presence ... It was incredible!

"You will soon understand what it is about."

"Oh, Ezahyel, you are here ..."

"Yes, I am. I know you have questions. I will answer some of them, but not all."

"Very well. I understand. So, to start with, who was that being we saw floating around in the air the other day?"

"To put it simply, one of your brothers."

"One of my brothers? Because there are many of them?"

"Ha ha ... you could say that. You do have quite a few. But I think it is still too early to really talk to you about this."

"OK! But at least tell me who it is. Where is he from?"

"He's from the Pleiades and he's part of the Ash'Tar Command fleet."

"The Ash what?"

"Ash'Tar Command."

"What exactly is it? It's strange, but that name rings a bell as well."

"Yes, and that's normal. You will gradually remember many things. You have known Ash'Tar for a long time. He is the equivalent to what you call a leader. But it is different from the leadership you know on Earth. An ambassador would be the most fitting word in your language. He has managed to bring together millions of souls—who have all volunteered—for one sole purpose: to accompany you. His love for humanity and your planet goes far beyond words and beyond your world. But it would be too long to explain this to you right now."

"Wow. I do feel a connection with him ... a strong and powerful connection, but I don't really know ..."

"You will remember when the time comes."

"And so, the being who came the other day—my brother— why was he there? What did he pass on to me?"

"He gave you information in the form of light. It is called Light Language."

"Oh, all right, that's why it was like a flash of light in my eyes? I feel I knew the code, without being able to put it into words, however."

"Yes, David. And that is natural. You actually know this language very well, but being a human does not enable you to integrate it fully yet. It will happen, but over a little time. Your DNA has to be re-encoded to integrate it again. It has already begun—it started when he transferred this information to you."

"So, you're saying that I know this language very well? From where? When?"

"I know you have many questions. But I won't answer them all."

"Yes, I know, I understand that it's up to me to remember.

But a little guidance or light on my path would be very welcome. Because quite frankly, it's not easy to untangle all this."

"I understand. Life in density is not a simple experience. And in that, we honor the choice you made. We honor you at all times. You decided to 'come down' here for one reason. Out of unconditional love. For the moment, it seems complicated because of duality and the 3D world, but you will soon remember, you will soon remember the lightness, the light ... You will remember who you really are."

"A little clue?"

"Kie'Teir."

"Pardon me?"

"Kie'Teir is your name. The name you had—have—as a high sphere being, as a light being."

Goosebumps ran through my entire body. My pineal gland started to vibrate very strongly and my crown chakra ... phew ... my crown chakra started to open wide and spin at great speed. So much so that it felt like it was sticking out of my head and kept growing endlessly. What was happening to me? I couldn't stand up. "I have to lie down" ... Ah, but I was already lying on my bed. What could I do? It was spinning around.

It is lucky that I don't suffer from vertigo. Ah, there! The blue luminous shape was back. Wow, it was spectacular, it was staggering ... It was even more luminous than the last time. Its hue was a little different as well. There were subtle nuances but I could not make them out clearly. I let myself be carried away in that crazy dance, as if I were carried away by a whirlwind. I was no longer aware of my body. Then, a kind of door appeared. I was immediately drawn to it. No sooner had I come close to it than I was somehow sucked in. Everything was moving even faster than before. I could make out stars, universes, and even galaxies going by all around me—it was dizzying, simply dizzying.

And then, all at once, there was a great white light, with a brightness like no other. Then nothing. The void. I couldn't remember anything else when I woke up, still lying on my bed. My father came into the room and told me it was dinnertime. Unbelievable. I had had the feeling several hours had gone by ... But it turned out that I had actually only been lying down for an hour. Ezahyel was gone. What an experience! What a journey!

I sat down for dinner with my family. I did not say a

word throughout the meal. At times, I could hear bits of their conversation. My brother and sister were talking about school, my dad about his work, but I must admit I was still hovering fifteen miles high ... I had traveled through space-time ... I was still quite shaken up ...

"Wow!" I said out loud without realizing it.

"What's wrong with you?" my dad asked.

"Huh? No, it's nothing ... I've had a tough day at school today and my mind just started wandering. Besides, I've had a great idea for a comic book ... The story is spectacular."

My father was a comic fan and asked me what it was all about. My mum used to draw too when she was younger. My siblings drew as well. So, they wanted to know a little more. I took the opportunity to tell them some things about this project—which wasn't really a project, but rather a subtle way of addressing the topic I had wanted to discuss with them for a long time.

"Well ... it would tell the story of a young boy who discovers he has some powers or abilities at the age of six. What's more, he is convinced he does not belong to this world. At the start, he doesn't know why he is here on this planet. He feels lost. He has many questions. Then, at the age of eight, he encounters somebody. A flying saucer flies above him then disappears. And then, he realizes there is a being in front of him. He has come for him. From then on, everything would change for that young boy."

"It is not bad. This would be a good sci-fi comic," my father told me.

"Yes, it's true."

"Where do you get all this?" my mother asked.

"I don't really know ... My imagination, I guess."

When I saw they weren't taking the bait, I switched off again. They knew my love for drawing and did not mind. At some point, I even heard something like "it's no real job," "what is the future for a cartoonist" in their conversation. They were right, somehow. I understood their point of view. Getting out of the beaten track has always been perceived as something hazardous or risky.

Even nowadays, it is still difficult to be a cartoonist or an illustrator and to make a living from it. It is a poorly considered passion and job. Even a cartoonist who has achieved a certain success has to sell thousands of comics to make a decent living from it. The author only gets a few cents out of each comic book sold.

Above all, he has to draw quite a lot to be able to keep on making a living from his art. In Japan, for example, mangakas do not have a regular eight-hour workday but work twelve to fourteen hours a day at the very least, seven days a week. Of course, working in the arts is most of all a passion, but it also implies many sacrifices. People do not realize it and it is a pity.

As far as I am concerned, I have always had a huge respect for these artists and their knack for drawing. Some of them have enthralled me with their talent. Sadly, the intuitive and creative aspect has no or very little place in this world. Yet art in general will be of considerable importance in the times ahead. It will even have a significant role in the fifth-dimensional world. I think I will talk about this further in Book 3.

Anyway, I wished them a good evening and went to bed. "How can I do this? How can I tell them about everything I'm going through?" I wondered.

"Do not worry about it for the time being. It's not the right time for them anyway," a familiar voice told me.

"Maybe … But I'd like to share this with them so much …"

"Oh, how we understand you. Right now, it is not time yet, but the time will come when you can tell them."

"Tell me, I still don't know who you are either. Ezahyel told me his name, but I still don't know yours. We've been exchanging for a number of years now and I don't really know who you are."

"Only you can know. I can't tell you anything. I can, in fact. But I won't."

"Why not? I don't understand."

"Have you already forgotten everything we have talked about so many times?"

"No, I haven't. Of course not."

"Are you sure?"

"Definitely!"

"Good. You remain confident in yourself and most of all, you remain who you truly are."

"Why would I change?"

"Oh, if you knew how many have said this to me and how many did not remain true to themselves, or even ignored me and pushed me aside, swept me away as the wind sweeps dead leaves. But the illusion of separation they can put between us does not matter, for in truth there is no separation. I will always be who I am. No more, no less. And my love will always remain the same, no matter what. It cannot be otherwise."

"I still don't understand who you are …"

"Are you sure? Or are you trying to convince yourself, or even ignore it?"

"I don't understand what you're getting at … I …"

"I am not getting anywhere. It's just that you convince yourself of things and make promises that, for many of you, you do not keep. This is not a judgment, far from it. It is an observation."

"I have the feeling you have been observing us a lot and for quite a while."

"You could say that … except that for me, time is only relative. Let's say that *I am* and I am who I really am in the moment … all the time. I am using these words, because these are the words you use and understand. In absolute truth, it is quite different. It even goes beyond your human understanding. There are things which are a mystery to you. And they will remain so. The mystery is what it is: a mystery."

"You're losing me a little bit here …"

"No, I am not. I have never lost you. But many among you are getting lost, however. Many have drifted away."

"What exactly do you mean?"

"It is a mystery … or maybe it is not. Only you can remember, David. Only you can be aware. And you know where to position yourself for that."

"In the heart."

"Exactly. And what is in your heart?"

"Love?"

"Yes! But indeed, there is much more than that."

"Much more?"

"Yes, there are feelings. And feelings are the language of the soul. And your soul is who you really are. In your heart lies your truth. That is, who you really are."

"Yes, I understand much better. It resonates … it vibrates in me. But what is my soul trying to do here?"

"It is not trying anything. It only wishes to be who it really is. What matters to it is only what you are while you are doing what you are doing, regardless of what you are doing. What your soul is 'seeking' is a state of being, not a state of doing."

"And what is it seeking to be?"

"You. Me. Us. Your soul and mine are only one, for as you know it, nothing is separate. Everything is connected. So do not do anything. Be. Just be. Be who you really are."

"Thanks."

CHAPTER IV

The Universe Is Vast

The universe as a whole, but also the entire cosmos in all its dimensions, contained within the Great Whole, is full of conscious beings and each one is driven by one thing—the urge to express and live fully who they really are.

To do so, it is essential to live and experience all aspects of physicality and immateriality, to understand and integrate them. The star nations have long grasped this and are striving to share this with humankind. For, as you know by now, the ongoing evolution process will enable us to reach the fifth dimension. This full integration can happen at any moment. As incredible or extraordinary as it may seem, more and more people are becoming aware or are awakening, more and more are remembering who they really are.

The more human beings awaken in large numbers, the more our civilization can begin to live as an awakened species, as a highly evolved species. It is up to you. Only you can get the world to move. Do not expect it to come from your rulers. The leaders of this world do not care about evolution and about who you really are. They care about keeping control and hence, power. How do they keep control? Through fear. For thousands of years, they have sown fear to enslave humanity, to dominate, and to get rich. So, we are kept in an artificial sleep through false beliefs, false precepts, false ideologies, and false laws.

But times are changing. The darkness is fading away to make way for the light. We are taking part in a great adventure that we would never have thought possible.

The Eagle Vision

If you could look beyond the Earth, beyond your condition as humans, beyond judgments, beyond detractors, beyond prefabricated patterns, beyond money, beyond politics, beyond mental constructs, beyond the rational mind, beyond fear, beyond suffering, beyond anger, beyond the darkness ...

You could see the vastness of consciousness. You could see how beautiful, loving, and limitless you are. You could see yourself as you truly are! You could see the greatness of your soul. Step back and see everything as a whole, in its entirety. See beyond duality, see beyond the illusion.

Have eagle vision.

And then you will see that everything is connected. You will see that we are all part of this Great Whole. You will see that nothing is separate. It cannot be otherwise. This is what the vision of the eagle has brought me. The eagle has been with me as far as I can remember. His spirit is pure wisdom.

He is a messenger. That's why he is so important in Native American culture and why it is the keeper of the East on the medicine wheel. The East is where the sun rises, where a new day begins. It is also the place of enlightenment. In many cultures, people turn eastward. They know instinctively, intuitively the natural and universal order of things.

You will later understand why this vision of things is very important to me.

Beyond Appearances

Back in school, a few weeks after the appearance of my Pleiadian brother, things had clearly not evolved at all. No one remembered what had happened. Not even Fab. I had to admit this was quite a tour de force. Who would have thought they used a sort of gas to pull the wool over our eyes? I was sure that sooner or later, someone would talk, someone would remember. Ezahyel confirmed it, their gas can only have a short-term effect on some people, or none at all—as with me.

In any case, I understood better the means they had at

their disposal and how they managed to nip things in the bud concerning UFOs and extraterrestrial presence. What could be done in the face of such powerful people?

"Just be yourself. This way, they won't get to you," Ezahyel said to me.

"Being myself protects me?"

"It does. The more you are in the heart, the more you are light ... and light they cannot touch."

"Is it really safe? Not that I have doubts, but what if a man shows up in front of me with a gun and is about to shoot?"

"If this is the case, then you have chosen it. Do not forget that all souls are connected and that they have a sort of contract with each other. So, if you have decided to choose that option and you take action, death will indeed be the outcome. Remember that any emotion of fear induces fear, including in your attacker. And you also have the opposite. If you react with love to him, your light will reach him ... but he does not have to accept it. He can always choose to shoot.

"Either way, everything will be perfect, in that you would both have acted upon your higher choices. And all these choices are made with love and out of love. But as a rule, with some exceptions, being yourself does protect you. You have experienced it before, haven't you?"

"Yes, that's true. Like that time when we were in a bar playing pool and a fight broke out. It quickly escalated. Everyone came to blows. I immediately created a cocoon of light around my friend and me. It was as if they couldn't see us. As if we had become invisible."

"Literally. That is what happened. In their eyes, you just weren't there, because they could not see you."

"Yes, but they knew we were there because four of them were waiting for us to finish our game to start theirs. So, how is that possible?"

"Let's say you faded from their view. Given the energies they were in—anger and even hatred for some—they just could not be in tune with love and light anymore. They were sinking into violence. In that case, the dark side makes you blind."

"Wow, I love the *Star Wars* analogy. I love these movies, you know!"

"Yes, I do, and that is why I alluded to it. For there are

messages in the movies indeed."

"So if I understand correctly, then Georges Lucas is a … messenger."

"Absolutely. Many people spread messages, whatever the means or tools they use. The message has to get through. Some people are there to disclose information. Just like you."

"Like me? Is it all that I'm here for? To disclose some information?"

"No, I did not say that either. Many things await you. And remember everything depends on the choices you make."

"Many things await me? Can you tell me a little more?"

"No, I can't. I won't. You cannot interfere with your freedom to be what and who you are."

"I understand," I said. I must admit I was a little disappointed.

"Do not be frustrated. On the contrary. Your path is lit."

The Spirit World

The week went by at a crazy pace. The end of the school year was just around the corner. Even if I too couldn't wait to get it over with and even though I shouldn't let it rub off on me, I felt a little twinge of sadness. So did Fab.

I saw Christophe more and more. We would go to each other's home every other time. On a Saturday night when I was invited to dinner at his place, he spoke to me again about spiritism. He told me that he knew a lad who wanted to hold a séance, because he wanted to communicate with a relative who had died a year or two ago. I agreed, while reminding him that it was not a game.

"Yes, I know. And I told him myself it was no joke. He is serious in his request."

"Well, OK. When would you like to organize it?"

"Tonight. He's coming around ten."

"What? You could have told me before!"

"I couldn't. He called me shortly before you arrived."

It was quiet during the meal. We talked about anything and everything. The end of secondary school was close, and Chris asked me what I planned to do next. I told him I needed to find a job, but not a permanent one because I had not done my military service yet. What boss would hire me knowing that?

"When are you due to start?"

"In January next year."

"Ouch. Yeah ... tough."

"Tell me about it! You know my aversion to weapons and violence ... I don't know what's in store for me there, but one thing is for certain, I don't want to go."

"No wonder! I ..."

There was a knock at the door. Chris got up and immediately went to open the door. Once our guest was here, Chris introduced us: "This is Guillaume. Guillaume, here's David, whom I told you about on the phone."

"Pleased to meet you," he said.

"Pleased to meet you."

"So, David, I hear you're an expert in spiritism?" he asked.

"Er ... no, I wouldn't go that far ... but let's say I've been practicing for a few years now."

I could not tell him, or Chris for that matter, that I could communicate with entities and with beings from elsewhere without using esoteric practices or rituals. They were not ready to hear that. Many people need a visual, material prop, so their mind and rational side are reassured. You never know.

Yet one thing struck me at once with Guillaume and intrigued me. He was indeed sincere in his request, I could see it in his heart. What struck me was the negative entity that was clinging on to him very closely. As if it did not want me to get to him. And what was even stranger was that I could not see its face. It was trying to hide it. But given its size and mass, I had my own idea about its real identity. Once again, I would not be able to talk about this. I would have to play it smart.

"Christophe told me it could be dangerous ..."

"Yes, indeed! It can be dangerous if we come across a negative entity—or an evil spirit as some people put it—during the séance. It happens quite often whenever people practice spiritism or any form of ritual, because they do not know who they are really dealing with. Let's face it, a lot of people are novices. Many also do it for fun, while others do it out of personal interest. And that's when it goes wrong, eight times out of ten."

"Well, you look like you know a lot about the topic. You know what you are talking about. And you're convincing. Nevertheless,

I do want to do it. I need to get in touch with someone. Is it possible to get in touch with him?"

"You mean your grandfather?"

"Oh! How do you know? Did you tell him, Christophe?"

"Oh no, I didn't. He only heard you were coming a couple of hours ago. I didn't tell him anything."

"That's just incredible. I can't believe it … How do you know?"

"I just do, that's all. I can't explain it to you, because I can't figure it out either."

"It's crazy. It could be …"

"Scary?" I finished his sentence.

He got goosebumps. A shiver ran through him from head to toes.

"Can you read minds too?" His voice was shaky.

"No, I can't. It's more of a feeling, I'd say."

"Does it happen with everyone?"

"Well, yes. The minute I see someone, I feel things … But I don't say anything, out of respect for their integrity and intimacy. I keep it to myself."

"Now I'm …"

"Flabbergasted?" I joked.

"Yes. No … impressed. I meant impressed," he said with a grin.

"Very well. Light-heartedness is good and beneficial. If everyone's relaxed, then we can get started."

After a short debrief to remind them of the proper conduct, everyone was ready. We proceeded in the same way as the previous time, that is to say we got some pieces of paper ready and once they were set up, we started the séance. At the beginning, everything went well. Guillaume's grandfather was indeed there. I chatted with him telepathically without the others being aware of it. He was delighted to see his grandson. He left after a while. I was about to stop the séance when something happened. The protection I had put around Guillaume shattered. The negative entity took advantage of this to take "possession" of Guillaume's body. His eyes rolled upward. He then said in a deep and raspy voice:

"This time, you're dead! We know who you are. You're done!"

CHAPTER IV

I must say it gave me the creeps. The others were frightened and ran out of the house. I had no choice but to react. I stood in front of him and sent him all the love and light energy I could. The "fight" lasted for a while. He resisted. I immediately asked my guides for support. A snarl was heard. Then in one fell swoop, Guillaume was thrown backward and fell against the wall behind him. He was unconscious. The entity flew off, snarling still, and then it disappeared.

I went outside to find the other team members. At first, they did not dare come back inside. Once I was sure the entity was gone, I had to tell them that Guillaume had been hurt and was unconscious. I needed an extra pair of arms to lift him up and put him back on a chair or a sofa. It must be said the lad was at least six feet, three inches high and weighed 198 pounds at the very least.

We were all around him when, after a good five minutes, he finally came to.

"What … what happened?"

"Don't you remember anything?" Chris asked him.

"Er, I don't know … I remember talking to my granddad during the séance … and then I sort of went blank … That's it, it's all dark. I have a headache too. A really bad headache. Has anyone got an aspirin?"

"There must be some in my mum's medicine cabinet. I'll be back."

In the meantime, I had given him a glass of water. He was very thirsty as well. Christophe came back with the aspirin tablet, which he handed to Guillaume. A couple of minutes later, he really got a grip on himself.

"Can someone please explain? What happened to me?"

They all looked at me without a word.

"Right. Are you sure you want to hear this?"

"I don't know … But go ahead."

"Well, sit tight. You may find it shocking."

After I told him everything in detail, everyone kept quiet, stunned and scared. I was anxious to reassure them anyway. It must have taken me at least two hours. Guillaume went home. He was still dazed, but he felt better.

I was about to take my leave of my hosts as well, when Christophe told me: "It's over. I don't want to hear about it again.

I'm done with all this."

"I understand. I understand it very well. At the same time, I warned you."

"Yes ... you did. What idiots we are!"

"No, you're not. Don't say that. Now you know."

"Yes. Ciao, David. See you soon!"

"See you!"

The Orion Greys

Jimmy Guieu[4] claimed this several decades ago now—among other disturbing disclosures he made: they are here, among us, lurking in their dens, huge underground camps hidden at a depth of several thousand yards. They keep an eye on us, attack us, and sometimes kidnap some of us ...

"They" are small beings from faraway worlds, those "Greys" who, thanks to the complicity of the high and mighty of this world, threaten to colonize, enslave, and even eliminate the human species. Other humanoids are said to have contacted human beings to warn them against the dangers facing the world.

Jimmy Guieu, who died on January 2, 2000, under very strange circumstances—I'll let you do your own research—was one of the only Frenchmen to openly reveal information about UFOs, extraterrestrial presence, etc. He was denigrated and ridiculed over and over again but he never gave up. He put his whole heart into it until the last days of his life.

In the 1990s, I read all of Guieu's books I could get my hands on. It is obvious that he came very close to the truth. And he was a nuisance, as you can imagine.

Yet, I want to make it clear that the Greys never actually acted on their own. They obeyed orders. And those orders came from much more powerful involutive entities: the Reptilian Dracos. I will tell you more about them as we go along.

As for the Greys, you should know that there are actually several "types" in their species: the Orion Greys, those from Zeta Reticuli, the tall Greys ...

---

4   Jimmy Guieu, *Nos Maîtres Les Extraterrestres* (Presse de la Cité Editions, 1992).

The Orion Greys are said to have been created by the Reptilians from the DNA of the Zeta Reticulans working for them. The Orion Greys are responsible for all the human abductions throughout the world—mine included. There have actually been far more abductions in France than we think. The purpose of these abductions has been to extract DNA, blood, sperm, ova, etc.

According to what I was told, they would devise a kind of liquid based on these human ingredients to feed themselves and they would absorb it through their skin—probably in a kind of bath, in a chamber, or in an incubator. They have also created hybrid races, who are genetic crosses between humans and Greys.

The Orion Greys can be of different heights. The ones I have dealt with were about four feet, three inches high. They don't wear clothes. They have no genitals and no digestive system. They are clones. Their hands have three fingers and their feet two toes. Their body is lean, with a narrow lower abdomen. Their head is large and so are their eyes, which are almond-shaped and covered with black lenses. Their mouths and noses are small. They do have a similar feature to the Zetas: their forehead is slightly rounded, which makes them look irritated or angry even when they are not.

They can be dangerous to humans. They are arrogant and act as they please, yet surprisingly, they are sometimes afraid and then they calm down. I have found out in my abductions that when you talk to them calmly and ask them to relax, they usually calm down.

They motivate one another on the pretext that they were made that way, that is to say arrogant, violent, and nervous. Now, not all of them are like that. Some rebel and change their view. That is how I was able to communicate telepathically with one of them. But I have to admit that it was a traumatic experience. At the beginning, I struggled and did not remain passive.

So much so that once, after they had just brought me aboard their ship, I disagreed with their behavior so much that they dragged me by my feet. I managed to get up and to hit the two Greys that were holding me. They fell to the ground. The other two Greys took fright and left. Those who were still on the ground were looking at me, haggard and scared. I started to run in the corridors of the ship, unable to find a way out. After a short while, they fell on me again.

I did not know then what I know now. I was young. I did not understand. So, why me? Why us? The universe is vast.

There were many unanswered questions. Man, because of his molding and his belief system, is scared of the unknown. However, the unknown is not that scary in the end.

France, let's face it, is one of the most narrow-minded, hermetic, and rational countries when it comes to these issues. I have experienced it. When dealing with so-called sensitive matters, obstacles are put in your way. Your phone is tapped, you are under surveillance, and you even get death threats. In a country where freedom is supposedly the keyword, you quickly realize there are boundaries you should not cross, chains you should not break. However illusory they may be, they are nevertheless there. I will soon come back to the moments I went through and which really affected me.

Regarding the Greys and my numerous abductions, I had to understand why. So, I asked Ezahyel.

"Dear David, all I can tell you is that there *is* a reason for this, that it is part of a 'Plan' that they have devised, and that this plan is beyond human understanding, at least as things stand. Know that you are taking part in something bigger than your human condition … something universal. For now, you have only put together a few pieces of the puzzle. You do not see the whole picture yet."

"Wait. Excuse me, what do you mean by something bigger?"

"Let's say that what you are experiencing now is also by choice. Your higher self made that choice, as agreed with those beings. You do not remember it just yet, but these are the facts."

"What? I chose this? I must be nuts! Why did I choose such a thing?"

"Haha! No, you are not nuts. Your current view of things does not enable you to see the whole picture. What is, is. And it is just marvelous."

"Marvelous? It is marvelous to be manipulated? To have blood and other substances extracted? It is marvelous to have your brain turned upside down? To have false memories? To be abducted every night or so? What is marvelous about all this?"

"Love. Unconditional love. But it is still too early for you to grasp the scope and meaning of all this. We understand your distress in your perspective, but don't worry, we are with you. We are always by your side. Soon, you will see things more clearly. Soon, light will be shed. Stay focused and put your awareness in your heart."

I could feel Ezahyel was about to leave.

"No, please wait a little longer."

"I have to leave you for now. I am called elsewhere. It seems of great importance. See you very soon, David."

"Ezahyel?!"

He no longer answered. How could I get out of this? Why would I agree to be abducted by these Greys? Out of love? I did not understand anything anymore. Why did I feel animosity if it was love? Yeah, right … It seemed completely ridiculous. Next time they came and fetched me, they would get to know me, I promised myself.

The Big Question

We were now two weeks away from the end of the school year. The closer the fateful day, the more Fab and I rejoiced but for my part, I had a knot in the pit of my stomach.

"Don't worry! We'll see each other afterward, I'm sure," he said to me.

Deep down, I knew it would not be the case. Sometimes, I can see and feel things before they happen. Fab, even if I had given him my phone number, or at least my parents' landline, as we did not have mobiles yet, was never going to call. This is how life is and I have accepted it without judgment, but with a slight disappointment all the same …

After all, feeling these things is human. And we had gone through so many things together in four years. He unfortunately did not remember all of it. Maybe it was better that way. Anyway, on our last day at school, I heard a guy talking with others about a subject that caught my attention.

"I swear! My uncle knows a guy who saw an alien float in the sky above the buildings," he said to his friends.

"You've got to be kidding. There's no such thing," one of them replied.

"Yeah, you only see that in sci-fi movies," another retorted.

"Er, excuse me. I couldn't help but overhear what you were saying. When was that?" I asked the key player.

"Several months ago, I'm not sure."

"In spring?"

"Yeah, I think so ..."

"Where was it?"

"Near Angers, I think. Why?"

"What exactly did he see?"

"My father told me. It was so precise. My uncle's friend is a lorry driver. He was on the road to deliver some goods to Angers. Shortly before he entered the town, he first noticed something in the sky. He thought it was a plane and he didn't pay attention at first. But as he drove on, he realized he was getting closer to what he saw. It seemed to be flying at very low speed. He was surprised and skeptical, so he decided to pull over to the side of the road as soon as he could. That's when he understood what it was. It wasn't a plane. He couldn't believe it even when he saw it. He thought it was a man and so he started yelling to him. The being turned around and slowly made his way toward him. The guy tipped over backward. There you go, that's all I know. Oh, no, he spoke of his eyes. He got a sort of flash of light when he looked at him. And he was wearing some kind of silver tights."

"That's him. We found him!" I said aloud.

"What are you talking about? Do you know about this, man?"

"Yes, sort of. Thanks for the information, anyway. Tell me, is there any way I can ask your dad for this mate's details?"

"I don't know. I can always ask him. But why? What do you want to do?"

"I can't tell you now. But if your father agrees, I'll tell you. Can you give me your phone number? As it is my last day at school, there's not much chance we see each other again."

"OK, no problem. Here it is."

"Can I call you this weekend? Will that be all right?"

"Sure. I'll talk to him about it tonight."

"Great! Thanks again."

As I slowly moved away from them, I heard one of the guys in their group ask: "Who exactly is he? Do you know the guy?"

"Yes and no. I've come across him many times, nothing more. All I know is that he does great drawings. Many people have talked about him in relation to his drawings."

I caught up with Fabrice, delighted to finally have some news about our "astronaut friend," who flew in defiance of the laws of gravity. It was the last school day and I have to say that I could not have wished for a better gift.

In addition to that, I had just got my two diplomas in Youth Training and NVQ Level 1 in roofing techniques. Yes, I knew it before the official results. I was going to become a roofer in the building trade, or not, as life and/or our soul sometimes makes us take a U turn without us necessarily understanding at the time where it wants to take us.

We had no more classes. Our last day at school was over and the summer holiday was starting, so we had some free time. Fabrice and I spent the rest of the day talking and exchanging. Then came the fateful time, the time to say good-bye. After a hug, Fab promised me again that he would call me. Without much hope, I replied slightly threateningly that he had better.

A page was being turned and not the least: four years. Four long years full of surprises and unexpected events. Four years of strong emotions, but also of aches at times. Friendships that started then broke up. The continuous training to get the diplomas was not always rosy. I have to admit that I did it grudgingly, knowing I would not earn a living in that field. But, hey, I had to start somewhere, since I could not go to art school.

And that damn military service lay in wait for me. What was I going to do there? I hated violence and weapons. So why? How could I avoid doing it? What would my role be in this highly hierarchical structure? This was the big question in my mind. What the heck was I going to do there? Goddammit! Or rather, what would I become among those soldiers? I was the opposite of all that.

"Do not worry, David. Everything will be fine. There is something in store for you there. Something you need to experience."

"Maybe ... but for ten months?"

Not long before, the government had decided to shorten the military service from twelve to ten months. It was good, I would say, but still too long.

"I am going to waste ten months of my life for nothing. It's going to be a waste of time. That's what it's going to be."

"What do you think your soul has chosen? Every single experience serves one purpose."

"Which is?"

"You will understand. Not right away, but you will."

"And you still won't tell me who you are?"

"You alone have to realize it. Have you forgotten?"

"No, I haven't. I know you can't hand us everything on a silver platter. It wouldn't do us any good anyway. It's up to each of us to become aware, to feel, to experience, and to live it."

"Absolutely. Otherwise, the result would be truncated. To give you an example, take someone who spends his whole life reading. He does it because he likes to read. But in the end, is the information he has piled up during all those years of any use to him? Does everything he learns or discovers through his reading really serve him?"

"I'd say it doesn't, in the sense that if the person does not experience things, they will be unable to understand and feel. Reading can guide you, enlighten you, but in no way make you live the experience."

"Absolutely. You've understood it all."

"We shouldn't experience things through others or through their works. Or try to conform and belong. We don't have to do anything, for that matter. We just have to be."

"Bingo! You are wise. Very wise. Do you know that?"

"Well ..."

"You have always been."

"Perhaps ..."

"Being humble is utterly honorable but take the compliments when they are paid. No need to blush, nor to feel ill at ease. It would limit you. Truth and love have no limits."

"Being whole, in short ..."

"Yes. Be who you truly are. All the time. Every minute."

"I understand. I really do."

"Yes, I know you do. And that is also why I love you."

These last words resonated in me like never before. It was sweet, soothing, comforting, and tremendously powerful at the same time. I had never felt such strength before. What was going on? It seemed so familiar ... and yet so far off.

"Who exactly are you? Why am I feeling this? I feel like I know you ... yet it is so vague, paradoxically. I am overwhelmed by great emotions and it's slipping out."

"This is normal. Remember that you are in a 3D duality-based system where everything is separate. Although there is no separation. Give yourself time to fully integrate, to be aware, awaken and remember."

"I want to know too much …"

"At times, you rush headlong like the ram. But there is no too much or too little. Things are as they are. I understand that you want to progress and evolve. You even have this feeling sometimes that you will run out of time. All the answers to your questions will not come to you at once. The fact that you remember who you are is spectacular already.

"Many human beings do not have this 'privilege' or 'chance.'"

"I admit it, of course. But I am not human. Even if I look like one. I don't come from here."

"It is true. Let's say that who you really are enables you to experience all this consciously and to remember many things."

"But I don't remember everything, right?"

"I would say that some things are dormant for now. You just need to remember, to bring them out of oblivion."

"How?"

"Remember you have chosen to come here and forget. That is the game. It is part of the experience. You have decided to voluntarily forget things about who you are in order precisely to remember who you truly are."

"Am I the only one?"

"No, son. Thousands, millions of others, have also made this choice."

My whole body was covered in goosebumps. My heart started beating against my chest. Son. He called me "son." What did it mean? Without me noticing, teardrops started to bead on my cheeks.

I did not utter a word. I could not anyway. I was in a daze. I could no longer feel the ground under my feet. All sense of gravity and density had gone. My mind started to fly. I had become an eagle. With loud, shrill cries, I reached the high-altitude clouds and started to sing with them. What a symbiosis with the elements! I could see everything. I soared, letting myself be carried along by the warm air currents. My heart, my mind, and my soul started singing in unison. I became one with the web of life. And what a web! Sumptuous, magnificent, spectacular, incredible ... Words fail me to describe the beauty of the Whole. Of this Great Whole, which we are all part of.

And suddenly, I heard two words resonate in the skies: Mitakuye oyasin.[5]

"Mitakuye oyasin." These words, although I did not yet know their meaning, resonated more and more within me. Where did they come from? What could they mean?

"Son, sometimes you have too many questions. You let a flow of thoughts engulf you. Your mind is scattered. Focus again. Stay as centered as possible. And then you will know. Then you will see, feel, and understand more than you do now."

"Is that all I have to do?"

"You do not have anything to do. You just have to be. And you can choose in each moment who you want to be."

"I can choose who I want to be?"

"Of course, you can! You do it every moment. You all do it every moment. You are unaware of it, that is all. But if you do it with full awareness, then it changes everything, absolutely everything. This will be explained to you soon. In the meantime, know that you are loved beyond what you can imagine or perceive."

I was at a loss for words and I told him this: "I love you too."

---

5   Mitakuye oyasin in Lakota means "we are all kin."

CHAPTER V

Emergence

"You are on the verge of rediscovering a reality that will satisfy your most magnificent quest, your most secret desire to surpass yourselves. The beauty in all things lies there and "awaits" your decision to fully express itself. So, how can I, as Creative Source, create the emergence of your full potential without overstepping your complete freedom? This is the paradoxical challenge uniting us."

In order to come together, according to the Creative Source's intent to see you be what you yearn to be, "reality" was created in different octaves and frequencies that are called "dimensions." Linearity as we perceive it in the third dimension pushes us to elaborate universal principles that coil around this very linearity, but linearity simply does not exist in the higher dimensions.

Then comes the time when those principles that our quantum physics is starting to explore or rediscover, such as multidimensional passages, parallel universes, or entanglement, become reality. It is difficult, then, in our own words and current perspectives, to bring this reality we are discovering in our movement of consciousness expansion back to this precise moment in our reality.

Is this getting a bit complex to grasp? Let's see it from a different angle. The three-dimensional matrix is based on three main structures:

- 1st—Duality: A dual mode of perception defined by the difference between light and darkness, positive and negative, true and false, hot and cold, up and down, causes and effects.
- 2nd—Linear Time: The perception of time as

moving only in a straight line, in one direction, and that is divided into Past, Present, and Future. The only present time existing in the third dimension is reactionary time.

- 3rd—The Rational Mind: It is our GPS in this 3D reality. It is the CPU[6] of critical and logical thinking, designed to make comparisons, draw conclusions, store information, calculate, and decide. Its purpose is to keep you safe and sound in the third dimension.

As a consequence, the third dimension is conditional and organized in a rigid density. Its atmosphere may at times be very heavy. It is regulated by a set of precise rules and it has many unique aspects, limits, mutations, and structures. It is a very stable biosphere, to be sure, but with little flexibility.

As for the fourth dimension, it has far fewer structures and rigidity. It is therefore more open and receptive, while offering a wide range of possibilities. It also favors choice and observation, providing a much more flexible platform than the third dimension and its well-known rigidity. The fourth dimension offers us a chance to redefine our reference points, to revise our old beliefs and to reach a new understanding of what is possible. The fourth dimension, which is a transitional dimension, enables us to be in the three-dimensional world, but without being part of it.

It is made up of the following:

- *The Present Moment*: This is the primary key. It is our power spot. Each present moment opens the doors to new beginnings and new experiences to be lived according to our own choices
- *Choice*: The freedom to make a different, conscious choice in each moment instead of reacting to what is manifested to you, is power. Your power.
- *Paradox*: Remember, the universe is full of them. It means flexibility. A fact that was true before may not be true in the next moment. By observing all this from the present moment, you will have the heightened awareness to make a different decision

---

6   Central Processing Unit.

at any time.

- *Alignment in Balance*: This is a state of balance which produces the presence of opposite forces without creating a reaction to what is before you.

So, you understand that in the fourth dimension, you have the present moment, the flexibility, and especially the choice to create all that you yearn for, while maintaining alignment and balance. If you create from the fourth dimension without transmitting love, your creations will remain stuck in the fourth dimension and will not be able to rise to the fifth. If you use these three pillars in balance, then they alone will allow you to create and recreate one or several completely different universes. You will then realize that you have access again to what was inaccessible when you came down to Earth in the third dimension. You will awaken your intuitive potential and your dormant spiritual abilities and thus regain the full use of your inner guidance system—the connection to your soul and to the Creative Source.

To this day, more and more people live in the fourth dimension and the often-rough episodes experienced in the third dimension will simply make way for renewal in your consciousness. You have probably already noticed and felt the gradual fading of memories linked to painful experiences, as well as other elements that are no longer in keeping with you, belonging to the past and to the third dimension.

These old ways of thinking and mental and emotional habits may still be taken into consideration. Needless to say that you will choose them less and less, thanks to the new perspectives of the fourth dimension. Soon, you will no longer choose them at all thanks to the fifth dimension.

You alone choose the experiences that you want to have and the particular circumstances of your existence. No one else does.

At what stage did you achieve the goals you had set for yourself? How many lives have you had in preparation for this one? Today, you have the outstanding opportunity to stay firmly centered, and especially so when your limitations, old habits, and other "weaknesses" manifest and threaten to bring you down again.

These weaknesses, which are related to your relationships, your work, or your money, will undoubtedly manifest. And then, you will notice that the "crap" starts over again. But you will be able to choose otherwise with this four-dimensional matrix. You will be able to make different choices altogether.

Your experiences, and everyone else's, are being amplified by the current Great Change, by this dimensional transition. It would therefore be very useful to connect to love and to let go of all that no longer belongs to you. By being centered within yourselves again in the heart, you will find it much easier to choose to let go of those out-of-date aspects of who you were.

If, however, you persist in your limitations and old habits, try to understand what they are. Otherwise ...

Well, you will fall right back into duality and three-dimensionality.

You can decide to free yourself now. The choice is yours and yours alone. If you choose to shed all that is outdated now, you will be brought to the doorway of the fifth dimension.

As I have explained to you several times before, the fourth dimension is a transition, a springboard—a springboard which will propel you to the fifth dimension.

The fifth dimension will open up an existence far beyond anything you can and could imagine. Life in the fifth dimension is completely beyond the influence of the mind, the rational mind, or the ego. They simply cannot realize or integrate the experiences of the fifth dimension. All is love. Everything is flowing. Everything is harmonious.

Even though a good many of us have already experienced this soothing and spacious sacred inner space, it is not easy to describe life in the fifth dimension in words and today's language.

It offers infinite possibilities that simple words such as joy, calm, bliss, happiness, respect, harmony, community, service to others, and creation can represent.

The density of the three-dimensional fabric is too heavy, rigid, and resistant to be harmonized to the light and airy reality of the fifth dimension.

It is simply impossible to go there with your limitations and all your three-dimensional baggage. It is equally inconceivable to enter the fifth dimension while keeping the low vibrations attached to the three-dimensional life experience.

It is as if you took a hot-air balloon and sent it to high altitude when it is too heavily loaded. What you are in the third dimension is just incompatible with the energy frequency of the fifth dimension.

Conversely, it is quite possible for you to be in the fifth dimension while existing in the third and doing so by creating from the fourth dimension.

You would be greatly surprised at the ease with which infinite possibilities blithely manifest in this clearer and faster multidimensional co-creation process. It is in the joy and sharing that we create with others, which again opens up the doors to infinite possibilities.

It is only from the experience in the fifth dimension that you will be able to create and recreate in love. Through this fifth-dimensional consciousness, not only will you remember who you really are, but what's more, you will create yourselves with full consciousness.

From thought comes speech, from speech comes action, from action comes reaction, from reaction comes creation—did you notice that reaction and creation are the same words, except the letter "c" is in a different spot?

To create or not to create, that is the question. All joking aside, it *is* a very good question indeed. What do you create? I have asked it many times to the people around me but few have managed to give me the answer so far. I hope you will find it. I do not pretend to be all-knowing or to have insider knowledge, far from it. It is just that I was asked this poser too and it took me some time to get it.

The Departure

"My life is taking a different turn," I thought as I waved good-bye to my parents through the train window. I did not know what awaited me in Lorient. The Field Marines' School opened its den to me for my military service. I did not feel ready to play soldier. The train was moving forward, leaving my former life behind me.

I took advantage of the journey to have creative thoughts. There are some experiences which I want to dismiss so I don't have to go through them. As I can't bear firearms and violence in all its forms, I needed to create the situation to avoid ending up in a commando unit or whatever group having to do with hardcore military training, and this at all costs. Crawling in the mud, doing drills in the forest with the bare minimum, and freezing at night … thanks, but no thanks!

During my three-day assessment,[7] I had tried everything I could to be exempted, to no avail.

"Fit for duty," I was told.

"Shoot," I thought. "I hope they'll send me to the navy." Because the land army was out of the question. Well, what do you think happened? I was sent to the Field Marines' School in Lorient, to the navy.

When I arrived at Lorient station, I took a taxi to my base. It was located on the left bank of the Scorf River, in the Lorient dockyard. Although the base was not far on foot, about two miles via the Chazelle Avenues, I wanted to avoid walking, loaded as I was with my big rucksack.

A few moments later, I presented myself at the entrance of the base. I had to show them my official papers. One of the guards came out of his gatehouse to show me the way in a serious manner. The base looked large, quite large indeed. On my way to my future quarters, I came across a commando battalion. They were almost all covered in mud and soaked to the bone.

"Dammit!" I thought. "What the hell am I doing here?"

"Do not worry, David. Everything is going to be fine. Everything is actually going very well."

"Ah, Ezahyel! Where have you been? I've been calling you for a while."

"Yes, I know. I was busy elsewhere."

"Can you tell me what the heck I am doing here? Because, even if this was planned by my higher self, I still don't understand."

"Would you question the choices of your soul?"

"No. Not at all, but …"

"Have you already forgotten its intention? Remember that even for a seasoned mind like yours, some mystery will remain. Otherwise, what would be the point of playing this game? Remember that you have come to this three-dimensional life

7   Translator's comment: all French conscripts had an initial three-day assessment and medical examination, which determined whether they were fit for duty and in what corps they would be called up.

sphere of your own accord and in full consciousness and that you have therefore agreed to forget who you are."

"Yeah, well, it pisses me off … I don't know what got into me that day."

"Do not worry, everything is going according to plan. According to your plan. Have faith."

Ezahyel had just left again. An officer escorted me and told me about the working rules and regulations of that base. I might as well say that he was already getting on my nerves. Maybe I had a problem with the hierarchy or the established order, or maybe even with both. It was going to be fun.

After finding my dormitory, I unpacked my things and looked around. The room was fairly big, with three bunk beds. It meant there would be six of us in this room. The showers were on the other side of the room and they were fairly spacious as well. We each had a locker to put our personal belongings in. I started putting my things away. As I seemed to be the first of my group to have arrived, I chose the bed which was next to the window. The door opened with a bang. The officer was escorting a newcomer and bidding him welcome. The lad seemed delighted to be there.

"Hi! I'm Max. I'm from Panama, but I'm actually West Indian, Guadeloupean, to be more precise. What about you?"

"I'm David. I come from Nantes. And I have several origins."

"Ah, great. You'll have to tell me about it, if you don't mind."

"Yes, no worries. I'll be happy to."

"Anyway, it's nice to meet you, David."

"Nice to meet you too."

"How long are you here for? Ten months? Or did you sign up?"

"I definitely did not sign anything. I'm just here because I have no choice."

"Yes, I understand. Military service, right."

"Yes, that's it. What about you?"

"I have signed up for eighteen months. I couldn't find a job. It's not easy for people like me to get a job. You know what I mean?"

"Yes, absolutely. I have friends of African origin at school. It wasn't easy for them either."

"Don't even talk about it. When you're black, it's hard to be accepted and ..."

The door opened again. This time, there were two other guys coming in. We introduced one another quickly.

Erwan also came from Nantes and Marc came from Auxerre.

"Wow! That's a long way to go," I said.

"Yep. It's a pain indeed. I will only be able to go home once a month. And to top it all off, I'm broke."

"Yeah. Tough indeed. I'm sorry for you," Max told him.

"Thanks, mate. Would anyone have a fag? I haven't smoked for hours, I have to have one."

"No problem. I'll go with you," I offered, handing him a cigarette.

"I'll come with you, wait for me."

And there we were, the three of us, Max, Marc, and I, having a smoke outside.

The first couple of minutes, we did not say a word. I was looking all around me. Honestly, the environment was not appealing. Buildings scattered everywhere, concrete and asphalt, the large naval hangar farther down, plus the atmosphere there. There was quite a mix of residual energies; it was hard to really make them out. There was fear, anger, hatred, and a whole bunch of negative emotions. Brrr, quite frankly, it almost gave the creeps. Luckily, there was a whole green, wooded section within that base, otherwise everything would have been grey, without any shades.

Then, all of a sudden, I heard Max speaking.

"Hey, are you all right?"

"Yes. Yes ... It's just that I was wondering again what the heck I was doing here. Don't you feel like leaving?"

"No," they answered in unison.

"Oh, I see. Marc, did you want to be here too?'"

"No, not really ... but I had no choice. I had no job and I was in a financial mess. I got out of school a few months ago. I didn't get my diplomas and I could not be on the dole. So, I might as well be here earning a little something than nothing at all. My mother couldn't pay for everything anymore. She's had to work part time because of her health issues. So there you go, you know the whole story ... I'm just ..." He had started crying. He must have had a lot on his plate, as they say.

Max and I tried to comfort him. After smoking a second

cigarette, he felt better. We went back inside. Erwan was having a chat with two other guys. So, the last lads in our room had arrived.

One was called Daniel and the other Christophe. After we had introduced one another, our staff sergeant burst into the room and said, "The mess opens its door in fifteen minutes. You will go and have dinner at seven sharp."

"Seriously, is it going to be like this every single day?"

"No, that's because we're new and it's the first day," Max replied to me.

So, fifteen minutes later, we were in the mess. It was crowded. We queued up. Many were staring at us.

"The greenhorns have arrived," we could hear left, right, and center. Some even burst out laughing when they saw us.

"Well, it's going to be a lot of fun!" I said.

"Yeah … you're right. I think it's going to be no cakewalk," Max retorted.

Once the meal was over, we decided to take a walk around the base to get a feel for the place. To be honest, their food wasn't great. We headed toward the relaxation area, which was located in the center of the base. I must say it was welcome. You could have a cup of coffee there, buy all kinds of sweets—they had two vending machines, and cigarettes. The good news was that they were cheaper than in civilian life, as they were tax-free. Marc bought two packs. He offered us a cigarette each.

No sooner had we come out than a siren started to wail. A fire engine rushed by us.

"Hey, they even have firemen here?"

"Yes, they do. They're soldiers, actually. They're trained to be a fire team. They also have their own police, the coast guard forces," Max told me.

"Well, you seem to be in the know."

"I asked them for information before I came here."

"You wanted to know a little more because you are enlisting …"

"Exactly. I needed to know a little bit about what I was getting into. There are quite a number of departments here, you'll see."

"Maybe, but in my opinion, we won't be given the choice. They will put us where they want."

"I'm sure they will!"

In any case, I hoped we would not be too far apart. We were starting to get on well already. Even if I knew we should not have any expectations and we should not get attached, it would still be nicer with friends. Ten months there was quite a long time, especially when it's something that's imposed on you.

Once we were back in our quarters, we chatted late into the night. It was going to be a rough wake-up call. At six sharp the next morning, we all *had* to be up, wash up, make our beds, and then have breakfast. After breakfast, there was roll call and flag raising. A routine we had to get used to. Everything I love!

We were given tracksuits in the colors of the base. We had to wear them every day until we were assigned to our respective posts.

Once the fatigue duty was done, the first day was off to a flying start with sports. We had to run and then do all kinds of exercises in a row. Finally, our instructors split our group in two.

When one half lay on the ground, the other half had to run over our abs. What kind of practice is that? What's the point of being trampled on like shit? I did not see the point in it and I found it disrespectful.

I was in the first group that had to lie down on the ground. Then, the other half came running and stepped over us. We heard shouts here and there. One guy even got to his feet abruptly, crying and yelling: "Are you nuts? I won't allow anyone to step over me!"

Let's just say he took a blow to his ego. That was understandable. For my part, I had no problem with my ego. I questioned the principle.

"Come back here at once! Come back here or you're going to be in trouble from day one," one of the drill sergeants shouted.

The guy kept on walking and grumbling.

"Go ahead, get out of here and you won't have any leave for three months. Did I make myself clear?" the officer told him.

"Don't mess around, man! Come back!" was heard in the group.

After stopping for a few seconds, he decided to come back to us, looking down. He apologized to the drill sergeants. But it did not pay off.

"Are you a man or a pussy? Lie down!"

We were asked to run and pass over him twice. By the time

I got to him, I did everything I could to avoid stepping on him. I disagreed with the way they were doing it and with the humiliation they inflicted on this poor lad. If it were like this every day, I guarantee many would blow a fuse.

"No, do not worry. They are testing your endurance," Ezahyel told me.

"Oh, I see, are you sure?"

"Absolutely!"

"Are you sticking around?"

"I am always here and I will always be."

"Thank you. Genuinely."

Anyway, they did not make us do humiliating drills again the following day. I do not know whether it was Ezahyel's doing, but he was right. I also know that they cannot interfere with our matters and act against our free will.

However, there are subtleties and I think that they sometimes whisper things into our minds.

The weeks went by fairly quickly. The end of the first month drew near. I was able to go home for the weekend. What a relief indeed to be back with my family again, and to have a warm and soothing environment! My parents asked me how it went. I told them everything down to the smallest details.

"What post will they affect you to, then?" my father asked me.

Shin At'Ha

"I haven't a clue yet. We'll find out on Monday."

"You'll let us know. Are there any phones on the premises?"

"Yes, there are some phone boxes. I've got to buy a phone card, by the way. A guy lent me his when I called you on Thursday to tell you I was coming home on Friday."

"OK. We'll go and buy you one tomorrow."

"No, that's OK, thanks. I still have some money left. And we are getting our pay next week."

"And how much is that?"

"Five hundred and fifty francs,[8] I think."

---

8   France still used the French franc at the time (1994–1995) since the

"If you need anything, please let us know."

"Yes. Thanks again."

It felt so good to snuggle up in my cozy home again. I went to my room to lie down for a while and enjoy that time.

After a few moments, a feeling of lightness and peace came over me again. I soon left my earthly body behind. My soul took me far away. At first, I did not recognize the place. The sky was crystalline blue-green. The mountains in the distance were red. The grass under my feet was blue. It waved lightly in the gentle, warm breeze. As I turned around, I realized that there were three moons in the sky. One of them was fairly gigantic. Clearly, I was no longer on Earth.

There was a kind of music or song in the air. Soft yet powerful notes rang. I vibrated with them. My whole being vibrated with this mysterious melody. I was drawn like a moth to a flame and headed to where the wonderful chant seemed to originate. I didn't have much time to grasp what had happened. No sooner had I thought about it than I found myself in the very spot where the melody came from.

I was inside a large circular room. I could see through it at three hundred and sixty degrees. In the middle was a huge crystal. The incredible notes emanated from it. I was not alone. There was a being there, who was very tall—at least nine feet ten—and whose skin was blue. He cut a fine figure despite his height. His gestures were slow, calm, and incredibly right. The way he moved was like a dance. So much beauty emanated from him. His vibration was gentle and filled with light. He did not seem to see me.

"But where am I? Who's this?" I wondered.

"You are in the Bootes star system. I am Arcturian. My name is Shin At'Ha."

"Oh, I'm sorry. I thought you could not see me."

"Do not apologize. You have nothing to be sorry about."

"How did I get here? I was lying on my bed on Earth, and all of a sudden, I was here."

"The crystal. The crystal called you."

"The crystal called me? I don't understand."

"I am going to tell you. But first of all, tell me what you are feeling. In your being, in your heart."

Euro was introduced in 2000.

"What I'm feeling? First of all, this world, your world, looks familiar … It's as if I knew it. Then, mostly, there is this melody. I can't explain it, but I vibrated with the melody sung by the crystal. I know these sounds … it is as if they entered my cells and modified or harmonized something in me. What does it mean?"

"The reason for this is that you have lived here, David. Among us. You have been part of us. You do not remember it yet, but you soon will, since the crystal called you. Your memories will resurface in a gentle way so as not to flood your mind with information. The crystal called you precisely because it was time for you to remember who you are. It is true that you have many aspects and experiences across the galaxy, but you are here now because of your soul's choice. You sowed many seeds to mark out your path so that you could remember. This is one of these seeds."

"Yes … I can already remember that … In fact, we know each other. Very well indeed. You are my brother."

"Yes. That's right. I am so happy to see you again at last. My heart is overwhelmed with emotions. Welcome back to your family."

Tears were running down my cheeks. Strong emotions were rising along with old memories. Scenes passed before my misty eyes. It was so intense I could not utter a word. Shin At'Ha had come to wrap me in his long arms. I do not know how long we stayed in each other's arms. The moment seemed to go on forever.

"It is time for you to go back," he told me.

I still couldn't speak. I did not want to leave this place, this other home. The idea of leaving it again tore my heart.

"Do not worry. Now that you remember, the connection has been restored. We are connected. We have always been. Go in peace, Zhel At'Ha. May the love of Source be with you."

"Zhel At'Ha?"

"Yes, that is what we called you."

"See you soon, brother. See you, Shin."

I was back on my bed. Well, I was no longer on it but under the sheets. It was dark. What time was it? Was I gone that long? Wow, what an incredible journey. I was still recovering, still reeling from the emotions. I got up to go to the kitchen and drink a glass of water. It was nearly eleven. My parents were still watching television.

"We tried to wake you up for dinner, but we just couldn't," my mother then said to me.

"Yes ... er ... sorry, I must have been more tired than I thought."

"If you are hungry, everything's in the fridge. You just have to heat it up."

"OK, thanks."

I was hungry indeed. As I sat down at the table, I thought about what I had just experienced. I still couldn't believe it.

"How many worlds have I lived in? Where do I really come from?" I wondered.

"There are numerous answers to that."

"Oh, it's you again. I was starting to think you were gone."

"Gone? I have always been here and I will always be. No, you are the one who was not listening."

"I beg your pardon?"

"That is right. You were not listening to me. Since you have been in the army, you have disconnected from me. You have cut the connection."

"But why would I do such a thing? And how?"

"Let's say that you let your feeling of rejection of your military service overwhelm you and that it cut you off from some things. Or, if you prefer, you put those things on hold."

"But I never intended to," I retorted.

"You did not, but remember that everything is linked and interconnected, and that some thought forms can, through their impact, close doors and take you away from your center."

"How can I prevent this from happening again?"

"Come on! You know how."

"By staying centered in the heart?"

"Absolutely! Do not forget it. Otherwise, you will disavow me."

"Disavow you? Why the hell would I do such a thing?"

"There is no such thing as hell. And you will disavow me. You have already done so before and you will do it again."

"I won't. I promise you I won't."

"Do not make promises you will not keep. Many have made promises to me and few have kept them."

"I don't understand. Is this a judgment? A reproach?"

"Nothing of the sort. Just an observation. I do not blame you for anything at all. You are living your experience and for this you are sincerely thanked. By no means will you be judged. There is no judgment, no penance."

"In that case, why share this observation?"

"Simply so you do not forget it."

"A reminder, in other words?"

"Indeed. Remember the circles. They keep turning. It is good to draw circles. That way, you can look at things from a different angle."

"Yes, just as it is important to take a step back to better discern and feel."

"Exactly. Stand above it all, like an eagle soaring high."

"Oh, I love the analogy. And I love the eagle. Do you know that?"

"Of course I do. Otherwise, why would I have used such words?"

"Sometimes, I feel that you know a lot about me, if not everything. It is a little unsettling ..."

"That's right, I do know everything about you. I know you very well. And you also know me, except you have forgotten."

"You know everything about me? But who are you? I have the right to ask you, don't I?"

"Yes, you do, but nothing forces me to answer you. You alone have to remember. To become aware. To wake up from that long artificial sleep."

"You mean it's as if I were in some kind of coma and that to come out of it, I would have to find the light in the darkness?"

"It is a beautiful analogy. But, no, I would say it is more like a dream within a dream."

"A dream within a dream? You are losing me again."

"You will understand all this soon, son."

After this beautiful conversation, I finished my dinner and went to the south garden to smoke a cigarette. And as always, I contemplated the sky and all those stars. What a magnificent sight. To think that all this stretched out boundlessly. How was it possible? Despite my great open-mindedness, I still found it difficult to perceive this vastness for what it was. As on Earth, we set limits, boundaries ... there in the cosmos, there is no beginning and no end. It makes you dizzy when you think about it, doesn't it?

Green Spaces

It was Sunday night and I was back at the Field Marines' School. Even though I still did not like being there, I was getting used to it. And the budding friendship with some of the lads somewhat warmed my heart. At least, we were in the same boat, we were not alone.

"Yes, I know what you are going to say. We are never alone, because there is no separation."

"Yes, son. That is good, you remember. And then, you did not cut yourself off. Congratulations."

"I take things in pretty fast, see?"

"Oh, but I know that you have great abilities. No doubt about it. And what's more, you anticipate."

"Yes, my pineal gland has started to tickle me."

He laughed.

"Very nice image, I must say."

"Thanks."

This exchange did me good. I had almost forgotten where I was. Max had just arrived. He asked me where the others were.

"I don't know. I haven't seen them yet. I just got here a little while ago."

"Shall we go to the recreation room?"

"Yeah, why not. I'll finish unpacking and be right over."

The next morning, we were all ready for the flag raising. It was the day we were to know about our lot. After the trumpet blew, our officer gathered us in a room. The verdict gradually came for each of us. Some of us went to work in green space maintenance, some others in mechanics or laundry.

My turn came round and my name was called:

"Sailor Rousseau, green spaces. Go to their workshop and they'll give you your outfit."

So, there you go, the verdict was revealed. The job was rather cool, plus I would be with Max and a few other guys I knew. "I'm doing pretty well," I thought.

"Wait, wait. You haven't seen it all yet," Ezahyel told me.

"What now? What's going to happen?"

"Do not worry. You will see for yourself."

"Oh, you and your mysteries ..."

He started laughing and I no longer heard him.

The following day, we were all at our respective posts. Our officer at the green space maintenance was a warrant officer in his fifties. He looked rather cool. He gave us our day's assignment: to go and pick the dead leaves and all the rubbish we could find, and then to mow the lawn.

There were quite a few of us in the team, a dozen or so. So, the tasks were divided up. I found myself with a lawnmower in my hands. There was much more work than we would have thought at first. We spent the whole day in that area of the base.

The week went by fairly quickly all the same and we picked up the pace in that post. The weekend came and as I did not go home, I got to know the guys in my dormitory better. On Saturday, we went to Lorient's city center. It enabled me to discover the town. We spotted a couple of nice restaurants and a bar. As for me, I saw an esoteric bookshop, which was really good as I would be able to go and buy a couple of books for the upcoming weekend shifts. Besides, the boss seemed very nice.

Sunday was fairly quiet and we spent it at the base. To enjoy ourselves and dodge the mess grub, we decided to go to the local Chinese restaurant for dinner. It was a nice, pleasant yet mundane evening. Back at the base, something unexpected was to happen. We had gone to the recreation room to meet the guys who had remained at the base.

When we arrived, they were chatting about paranormal phenomena and UFOs. At first, I listened to them without interfering too much in their conversation. Some of the things I heard made me laugh inside. Some of them did not know what they were really talking about. One of them looked at us and asked: "What do you guys think? Have you ever seen UFOs?"

Max spoke first and candidly announced: "Yes, I've seen UFOs two or three times in Guadeloupe. It's my homeland. I was on the beach with my family one evening, and we had a barbecue, with grilled fish and a bottle of good rum. Then, at one point, a strange light appeared above the ocean. It did not seem to be moving. It twinkled brightly, changing from white to blue. Then, it started to grow. It was heading toward us. Some of us took fright, not knowing what it was. We did not even have time to hide when it flew over us at very low altitude, then it disappeared in a second without the slightest noise. All I felt as it passed by was some air moving as an indirect result. The following evenings, we saw it again at the same spot above the sea, only to disappear again."

"Did you find out what it really was?"

"We didn't and to be honest, I don't really want to know."

"What about you, David?" Daniel asked me.

"Well ... yes, I've seen some UFOs as well, many times actually. For example, one summer night, I was sleeping under the stars with a friend. We were watching the sky. Then all of a sudden, some lights started to appear right and left. They were twirling around in all directions. Manu was astounded and asked me about them. I told him they were not from this world. We went on scrutinizing them for a good five minutes. Then they all disappeared except for two of them. We soon understood that they were heading our way. I don't remember what Manu mumbled at that point, but in any case, both three-feet-three-diameter spheres flew over us. They were completely luminous and green. They floated there above us without making a single sound. Then, they went back upright at lightning speed and disappeared at higher altitude in a kind of luminous white flash."

"Wow! You see! I tell you there are more people out there seeing this kind of thing than you think," Daniel said to the others.

We went on chatting on these topics for a long time. When I saw the reluctance and doubts some had, I did not go into more details. To round the conversation off before we went to bed, I told them: "Anyway, guys, don't forget where we are. Better avoid some topics and remain discreet."

The Holiday Camp

Several months had gone by and I had to admit everything was going fairly smoothly. I had found a certain balance in my new life in the military. Bonds had strengthened with some guys more than with others. Not that they had become friends. They were just my mates and I was fine with that.

It was April and one morning, as we were getting ready for work, the warrant officer called me and invited me to meet him in his office.

Once I was in his office, I realized two other guys were there as well, waiting.

"What's going on?" I wondered.

"Morning, gentlemen! I've called you in upon the command of my superiors. We have plans for you. I strongly advise you to accept these offers, because many would like to be in your shoes."

I was puzzled and immediately asked: "What is it about, sir?"

"A month's holiday, all paid for. Are you interested?"

"I beg your pardon?"

"Over the school holiday, all the children of the soldiers on this base are sent to camp. These camps belong to us. Every year, we hire outside help, such as activity leaders, cooks, etc. We are short of staff in three of our camps. Are you in?"

It did not take us long to think about it and agree. You would have to be crazy not to seize such an opportunity.

"I'm warning you, however. Irreproachable manners and attitude are demanded. Don't make the slightest blunder. I'm counting on you. Is that understood?"

"Yes, sir."

"Good! Very good."

"Excuse-me, sir ... but why us?"

"Because of your good manners and behavior. You are discreet. You do as you are told without dragging your feet. So, do me a favor and be on your best behavior once there. I expect no less of you."

"Yes, sir."

"What exactly will our job be?" one of the two guys asked.

"So you, Sailor Jusseaume, you will be a commis chef. Sailor Guibert, you will be an aide-de-camp. And you, Sailor Rousseau, will be a driver. Your mission will be to drive the manager of the Gâvre peninsula camp on all her trips outside the camp. Is it OK for everyone?"

"Yes, sir."

"Very well. You may leave."

"Have a good day, sir," I told him when I left.

"Wait, Sailor Rousseau. I have to talk to you."

I wondered what it was now.

"Would you like to join the fire team?"

"Of course I would! Why?"

"One of the new recruits was not up to the task. He threw in the towel during the drills. Besides, we'll need a driver for the fire engine. You will obviously take the heavy goods vehicle driving test at the base. We have our own driving school. Any questions?"

"Yes, sir. When shall I start?"

"Next week, you will be transferred to the laundry with Sailor Lenoy. It will enable you to get your HGV license, so your absence does not disrupt your former team. The laundry room is right next to the security command post."

"What about August? How is it going to work out? I will be at a holiday camp for a month."

"Yes, that's right. It's been planned too. There will be two of you taking the HGV license. It will enable you to take shifts."

"Very well. Thank you, sir."

"You will be given the orders in due time for the August mission."

"Thanks again, sir."

It was unbelievable. I was about to change jobs, get my HGV license and, icing on the cake, have a free month's holiday at public expense.

"So, didn't I tell you that some things would happen?" Ezahyel asked me.

"Yes. You were right, my friend! That's great!"

"And you have no idea of what is to come."

"Pleasant or unpleasant?"

"Please be patient. Be patient."

CHAPTER VI
The Tearing of the Veil

The unique opportunity before us has always been seen as a possibility in our time. In co-creation with highly evolved beings and light beings, we finally have this possibility to create a new life. It has been yearned for by the most passionate hearts among us—the hearts of these souls that have come here to realize the dream within the dream. The dream is a unique and spectacular experience.

As the veil of the third dimension is increasingly torn away, the illusion clears more, leading humanity on the path back. Back to love. Back home.

Some will take a direct route, some others—less conscious—will take a diverging path, but all will eventually return to love. Because it is what we are, regardless.

Those who, by choice, are less awake, will take a longer path that will not lead them to the higher dimensions but rather to places where they will have the opportunity to remember who they really are, so that they can be conscious again and follow the great change. By doing so, they will in turn be ready to enter the fifth dimension.

For sure, some people we know and love may not be passengers of this train on the three-dimensionality track. We have to accept it and not be afraid for them. For, yet again, this is a question of choice. And all choices are made in love by the soul. So out of love, we will also accept their choice.

Remember that *you* chose to leave the "Mother House" to go down into the third dimension. You made that choice because the Creative Source wished to live multiple experiences so as to know itself better and thus, to recognize itself as such. It was only natural that it asked for volunteers. Guess who stepped to the front of the stage, made his or her way through the others, and shouted out: "Send me! I'm a volunteer. Pick me."

Well, you did. You, who are reading these lines.

The Source was delighted. It smiled and then told you: "I need to tell you what this third dimension really is. To start with, it is very dense. Duality reigns supreme there. It is also very dark. When you go down there, you will forget everything. You will forget who you are and who I am. You will go through contrasted experiences. You will put on many costumes and masks and you will be confronted with a wide variety of choices. In experimenting all this, you will have a heavy weight on your shoulders and over your head. And as you move through that darkness, you will seek and seek your way back."

"I will take up the challenge. It sounds like a stimulating experience," you said. You were a great many and you were happy to choose this new adventure ahead of you, despite the difficulty ahead.

As jolly as ever, you asked: "Concerning this darkness, how deep can we sink into it?"

"As deep as you wish," the Source answered.

FUSCO

I was back at the FUSCO[9] base after a weekend with my family. I told my parents I would join the naval firefighters team and that they would have me take the HGV driving test to drive the fire engine. My father could not believe it. He was proud. He asked me to take some photos of the team and of the truck when I could. When I also told them that I would be the driver for the director of a holiday camp throughout August, it left them speechless at first.

Looking back, I still could not believe it either. Could it be that I also had a lucky star, as they say?

"No, it has nothing to do with it," Ezahyel told me.

"What is it, then?"

"Those are your own choices. The choices you made in the higher dimensions and which come to life in this one."

"Wow! I had almost forgotten. So, I had chosen to experiment

---

9   Shortened form of fusiliers and commandos.

this or that according to what I go through, here in reality."

"Absolutely, yes. Except that what you are experiencing is not reality. Only a dream."

"A dream? But what does it mean, in the end?"

"You will understand. Be patient."

"In any case, I thank you for everything, Ezahyel. From the bottom of my heart."

"You are welcome. Thank you too."

I took my car to get back to the base. My very first car was a Peugeot 104Z. It really ran well and I liked that vehicle—just as everybody likes their first car, I guess. Driving provided me with more freedom than having to go to the station and waste time waiting for the train. I would only take the train once a month from then on, with the free train ticket the military gave us.

I came back a little early, before dinner. Erwan told me they were all going to the Chinese restaurant next door and that I was welcome to join them if I wanted to. I accepted his invitation. When we got there, we realized that there were some guys we did not know sitting at our table.

"Yes, these are the guys from the dormitory opposite ours. I don't know what positions they have, but I've seen them before," Erwan told me.

"Oh, very well. Thanks for the information."

We all ordered the same dish, following the advice of the regulars. It turned out to be very good indeed. While I was chatting with Max, Erwan called out to me:

"Listen, David, the guy in the middle, here, is talking about things you told me about. He's talking about EBEs."

"Really?" I asked, startled.

So, my attention was caught. And I listened to everything he said, without taking part. He seemed to know what he was talking about. He was asked questions, to which he answered calmly and passionately.

It was time to leave the restaurant. This was really a very good evening. Besides, I did not expect anyone to talk so openly about EBEs, or Extraterrestrial Biological Entities. We do not know where the term EBE comes from. Some claim it was invented by the American government and NASA to refer to aliens. Others say they invented the term to name the entity that was found alive in the famous Roswell crash. In any case, I liked the word. Besides, it had often been used by Jimmy Guieu. But how come this guy knew it? There was only one possible explanation: he was interested in UFOs, and very closely at that.

The next morning, I got ready to go to my new job. The warrant officer took me there. Once inside the premises, he showed me the machines—washing machines, clothes dryers, and vapor pressing stations, and then he introduced me to the person in charge. What a surprise to see that it was the same guy who had talked of EBEs at the restaurant the night before.

"Now, that's awesome!" I thought. "I wanted to talk to him. It couldn't have been handier."

Strangely, he seemed withdrawn at first. He hardly said hello to me.

"Don't worry. He was used to being on his own here," Ezahyel told me.

"Oh, and here I am breaking his routine," I answered.

"True, but know that everything is going to be fine."

"All right! If you say so!"

Once the warrant officer had left, I introduced myself briefly. I then learned he was called Olivier. He started explaining how the machines worked. I decided to take the bull by the horns and cut to the chase. "Please tell me, Olivier, may I ask you a question?"

"Yes, go ahead," he replied evasively.

"Last night at the restaurant, you talked about EBEs. What exactly do you know about them?"

A smile suddenly broke over his face. A glint came up in his eyes.

"You're interested in them too?"

"Oh, if only you knew! For many years, actually. So, tell me everything. If you agree, of course."

We chatted so much that in the end, we did not see the day go by. I had a different man before me compared to this morning. He had opened up, and the least you could say was that he was very interesting. He conducted personal research on UFOs and alien presence. He himself had seen some on several occasions. He was a genuine enthusiast and sought the truth through all this—his truth. And above all, a strong friendship would bloom between the two of us. I thank the source for this "gift," which was to make the remainder of my military service much nicer. I did not know what was in store for me. We did not know what was in store for us both.

Anyway, the following week, I also started my HGV driving training. Every morning, I went to the driving school on the base, immersing myself for two hours in basic mechanics, theory, and practice, as well as the Highway Code. The remaining two hours were devoted to driving. I really enjoyed it. I liked discovering new things. And I still do today.

One Monday morning, Olivier came to tell me about a new UFO sighting. It had taken place over the weekend in Lorient. He thought that the guy who had reported it had disappeared since Sunday morning. As if he had vanished into thin air. No trace of him remained. He was both astonished and horrified when he told me about this story.

"If you want, we'll do a little investigation," I told him.

"Yes. It would be good to know what really happened. You told me you were used to investigating, right?"

"Yes, indeed. But we'll have to do it discreetly, in particular considering where we are."

"Yes, I understand. Do you think the military on this base are hiding something?"

"There's no doubt about it. At least as far as the senior officers are concerned."

"So there really is a global plot concerning the existence of EBEs and UFOs?"

"It's much more complex than that, actually. I'll explain things related to all this, Olivier."

"Thanks. I'd love you to."

"However, let me say it again, we need to keep it quiet."

"Absolutely."

As I left for the driving school and wished him a good morning, he asked me: "Shall we talk about all this tonight? We'll leave the building and go to the ocean to have a bit of peace and quiet."

"Yes, if you want. No worries. See you later!"

"Bye, David! Good luck with your driving test!"

"Thanks. Ciao!"

Secret Base and MJ12

That night after we had dined and put on our tracksuits, Olivier and I went to the base's end. We had found a nice spot to sit before the sea. Just as I expected, Olivier asked me some questions, lots of questions, in particular about the role of governments and the secrecy they set up around everything related to extraterrestrial presence on our planet.

I explained to him that it all actually started in Germany in the 1930s—at least in our modern civilization. Because the truth is, it all started thousands of years ago with the arrival of false gods in Mesopotamian culture. Hitler and some secret societies like the Vril and Thule already worked on new technologies such as antigravity and other exotic technologies. They had managed to manufacture the first human, saucer-shaped spaceships with the help of a medium called Maria Orsic, who claimed she communicated with aliens from Aldebaran, and of Winfried Otto Schumann.

In fact, we know very little about Maria Orsic and the Vril, as so much information is shrouded in mystery. No documents confirm Maria Orsic's activities and it is even truer of the Vril secret society. The latter is said to have been founded in the late 1910s. It is actually as if all the information about Orsic, the Vril, and Schumann's involvement had been painstakingly eradicated to leave no trace. It must be said that it was the first secret space program to be launched in our time. It is easy to understand why such information would have been carefully kept hidden by secret societies in Germany and around the world, then classified as highly confidential by all the governments of the world afterward.

But I will come back to this later. In the meantime, you may research Maria Orsic on your own. What I have to say about her, based on some experiences I have had with her—she is still alive indeed—will seem very different from what some people say and/or claim about her.

Still, when I told Olivier that involutive entities had come to Earth a long time ago and that they were behind all the beliefs, but also all the dogmas, religions, and the Babylonian system, he was not that surprised. He then asked me questions about the MJ12. Operation Majestic-12 is a TOP SECRET operation of highly confidential information and intelligence.

The management of the project is under the control of Majestic-12 (Majic-12), a group which was established by special, classified executive order of President Harry Truman on September 24, 1947, on the recommendation of Dr. Vannevar Bush and Secretary of Defense James Forrestal. The members of Majestic-12 were named as follows: Admiral Roscoe H. Hillenkoetter, Dr. Vannevar Bush, Secretary of Defense James V. Forrestal, Dr. Jerome Hunsaker, Mr. Sidney W. Souers, Mr. Gordon Gray, Dr. Donald Menze, General Robert M. Montague, and Dr. Lloyd V. Bernker.

After telling him all I knew about that secret group, we decided to call it a night and go to bed. Olivier, who was insatiable, would have liked to continue our conversation, but I reassured him that we still had many months to tackle the subject extensively. When we arrived at the dormitory, I realized that everyone was already asleep. I did not make any noise so as not to wake them up and I went to bed myself.

Spirit's Call

All the experiences I had had so far unfortunately did not provide me with all the answers. Even though it is true that I had privileged relations with guides and star brothers and sisters, it was as if something were missing. As if I could not pinpoint what was most important. Something still eluded me ... And it had something to do with who I really am.

I then started to do some research and bought a bunch of books on all kinds of subjects: books about spirituality, paranormal phenomena, UFOs, wisdom, and even myths and legends ... for naught. Some things resonated with me, but without necessarily really making me vibrate. All these books gave me little clues, but nothing tangible. I was putting the puzzle together, but the key pieces were missing.

Then, one day, I came across a book about the Native Americans (First Nations) and their way of life. It was an electroshock. The more I thumbed through it, the more it spoke to me. Something vibrated in me. There was a sort of echo in my heart. I simply could not explain it in words. It was as if old memories resurfaced. I understood at that point that I had found my way back ... long forgotten, long lost.

All I had been feeling since I was a kid was then confirmed by those books and the spiritual teachings of the Native American wise men. I understood better my ability to see in time-space (from a shamanic perspective, it is called Eagle Vision). I understood better what my soul was trying to tell me when I discovered Black Elk's and Fools Crow's books.[10]

Everything became clear and bright. The final revelation came when I discovered the Hopis' prophecies—I don't remember what book it was, I lent it and it was never returned—and in particular the Rainbow Warriors' prophecies. Shivers ran down my whole body and tears started beading down my cheeks. I was speechless for a long moment, taking it all in the best way possible.

Then, I realized I was flying in the skies. Clearly, I had become an eagle again. Something strange then happened. It was as if I were flying up the space-time spiral, the same way the eagle soars in updraughts. I was going back in time. I saw the installation of electricity, the first cars, then the horse-driven carts, the first trains ... then, the endless plains, whole villages made up of teepees.

Then all of a sudden, there was a kind of tearing, the sky got darker. It was winter. It was very cold, given the buffalo hide blankets worn by the natives in that village. I could feel their anxiety. The air was electric. Despite the villagers' great love and respect for all things, I felt that ... It was as if they knew that something terrible was about to happen. Night had fallen, the snow had started to cover everything. The fires were tended inside the teepees to keep the heat up.

Suddenly, a cry went out in the night. There was something scary about it. The disoriented villagers woke up and went out of their homes. From that point on, the first gunshots were heard. The panic-stricken Lakota Mnicoujous started shouting to all the tribe members that they were under attack. They started running

---

10   The Sacred Pipe: Black Elk's Account of the Seven Rites of the Oglala Sioux (as told to Joseph Epes Brown). (MJF Books, 1997); Fools Crow's Wisdom and Power—Red Cloud, published by Thomas E. Mails, September 1, 2001, by Council Oak Books (first published October 1, 1980).

in panic to escape their assailants. A huge feeling of sadness engulfed me. I could see that the whole camp was surrounded. There were at least five hundred soldiers of the United States cavalry.

There seemed to be no way out. I saw men take children and elders out of their teepees and protect them, trying to find a way through. The soldiers went on shooting. We could also hear cannon shots. They left this people no chance. The cries of women and children could be heard over the incessant firing. Then, I was drawn to a man who was part of a small group who, by some miracle, had made it across the shooting ground and was guiding the survivors, to try and get them to safety behind the hills. My consciousness suddenly merged with this Lakota. I quickly understood that it was actually me. I shouted at the people I was trying to protect: "Come on! Come on! Run!"

I did not look back, but I could hear horses coming up behind us. Bullets whizzed by me. I saw a child collapse. Then a woman. And then, like a thunder clap, I felt a terrible pain in my back. Then a second one. I felt my body fall down with all its weight on the frozen ground.

With a start, I returned to my current body, not without difficulty. I had trouble catching my breath. Tears streamed down my cheeks. I was speechless again before such misunderstanding and cruelty. "Why did they do that? They massacred women, children, and old people in the middle of the night, while the village was asleep. They couldn't even defend themselves. It's a genocide, plain and simple. That's what it is."

My mind was in turmoil. I did not know what to do to calm it down. I had just relived a scene I had once gone through and it was terribly painful. It is tough to be shot twice in the back while running for cover and protecting your family members, without really understanding what is going on. On top of that, my back hurt. I felt I could feel the bullets inside. Oh, but could it be that? Every year, at the same time, I had pains in my back that came and went after a few days. I could never figure out why …

"Son, don't you understand?"

"Ah, is that you? Well, no, I still don't get it. Can you shed light on this? Because now I'm between anger, hate, and a desire for revenge … and I do not like those low-vibration energies."

"Having this kind of emotion is understandable. It is human.

Tough, I grant you. You know what you have to do to transcend this."

"Put myself in the heart? But I am, damn it! Aren't I?"

"Yes, you are. But there is one thing you have not done."

"Oh, I'm not in the mood for your mysteries. Can't you see I am in pain and still recovering? I'm sorry, but I was cowardly shot in the back, as were so many of my people, for that matter. How would you like me to experience it?"

"You do not have to endure it, or at least, you no longer have to. Can't you see you are still going through that moment? Refocus on the present moment and take a step back, shall you?"

"OK! I'll refocus and soothe all those painful emotions."

"Breathe in deeply and out slowly four times. Then, watch things from a distance as a spectator and not as the actor you once were. What do you understand? What do you feel?"

"Oddly, here and now, I feel love. A great love coming from that village. Each person inside the teepees vibrates in love despite the climate of war. They are united in the heart, respecting one another and everything around them. They have a great love for Mother Earth. It is indescribable with words, but it is magnificent. They protect themselves from the oppressor to preserve their way of life, their ancestral knowledge, their sovereignty, their freedom, and their being one with all that is. They are conscious of living fully who they are. The invaders are not. They are the opposite. They only think about power and about personal wealth. They do not understand us. We are not materialistic but spiritual. They hate us for that. They call us savages and yet, they are the ones invading our lands, destroying all they can and taking what they need. We understand that it is the end of a time. This was predicted by some shamans and by White Buffalo Woman. The five hundred nations would lose their lives and their freedom to be who they really are at the expense of their white little brothers. Out of love and acceptance, they would let themselves be herded onto reservations. They would be forbidden to pitch teepees, dance, sing, speak their mother tongue in the belief it would kill them at the root. But the red spirit—Native American—is rock solid; grandfather stone. They just put an end to the balance by forcing Native Americans to live the white man's way. For we are the Guardians of the Earth. They are not aware of it in the least. They are unconscious. Yet at the same time, I don't hold it against them. I mean, it was inevitable. It was bound to happen. Now I see who is pulling the strings behind the scenes and I have a better understanding."

"Very good, son. You have just seen the bigger picture. Taking a step back is a good thing to perceive the whole fabric and all that is being played there. Nonetheless, are you ready to forgive them? Are you ready to forgive yourself?"

"Forgive myself and forgive them?"

"Yes. That is what it is about, son. To forgive others and to forgive yourself is to love yourself. To love yourself fully and unconditionally."

"Pfew … That's not going to be easy … I'm still angry and sad right now."

"Need I remind you that, no matter what, all is but love? Everything is perfect in the moment. Your souls, out of love, have chosen these experiences, however dark they may seem. It is all part of the plan."

"What plan?"

"Rescuing your planet and making sure humankind becomes an awakened species."

"No less? Well, then, please excuse us. There are some awakened beings. There has always been. But they are killed. They are eradicated from the face of the Earth. How can we deal with these demons? It has gone on for too long. I also understand the suffering of our Mother Earth better. She is weary. She can't take it anymore."

"I understand you, son. But be aware that things are changing. Marvelous things are coming. You will go through disruptions, to be sure. Many of you will be shaken, very shaken up. But this is only a prelude."

"A prelude? A prelude to what? When? How?"

"Be patient, son. Be patient. You will get some answers."

"May I ask you something all the same?"

"I am listening."

"What I relived earlier, when and where was it?"

"I will answer this with two words: Wounded Knee."[11]

"Wounded Knee?"

---

11   On December 29, 1890, in Wounded Knee, South Dakota, one of the largest massacres took place. About 300 Lakota Mnicoujou were killed by the 7th US Cavalry Regiment.

"That is right."

"And how do you explain the pains in my back?"

"Cellular memory."

"Cellular memory? What's that?"

"Let's say your mind has stored things in its memory and it remembers them."

"Wow, that's insane. Thank you. But tell me, are there any other painful things like this my mind is going to remember?"

"Yes, some. But it will also remember wonderful things."

"Phew, I'm feeling better."

"You're welcome."

"Thanks again for everything. I feel lighter already."

"Indeed you are. But you have one more thing to do."

"Yes, I know. See you soon. I love you."

"You are also loved beyond words."

A Mysterious Apparition

Life continued on the base. Monday had just flown by. Olivier and I had talked about the secret governments, or deep state, and their involvement in the biggest lie in human history. He had understood that he had to unlearn all that he had taken for granted. The edifice built and implemented by the world elite is just an illusion. It is only there to control and enslave the masses, and above all, to keep them in a deep sleep. They do not want you to awaken, to become conscious, because you would regain your sovereignty. You would be free again. And they do not want that.

So, they decide for you, constantly setting up laws, rules. They do anything to put out the smoke and mirrors. They decide in your stead and judge whether it is good or bad for you. Be it through religions, dogmas, institutions, history, science, etc. They do their utmost to keep you in separation and duality and in particular, they do everything to keep you tightly bunched up together in the sheep herd, in order to prevent you from thinking, from becoming conscious and from being who you really are.

By being fully who you really are, you get out of the herd, you become a free spirit and thus, you are out of their control and out of reach and that is something they do not want. Many of those who have left their artificial matrix have been considered traitors, terrorists, madmen, rebels, or the rejects of society. Many have been threatened and even killed. Becoming a free thinker again comes at a price. But no matter the price. I'd rather be thought of as an eccentric or a lunatic than bury my head in the sand. As such, the warrior in me expresses himself and refuses to be deprived of his integrity and freedom. He refuses not to be who he really is. So, I do not agree with their game and domination.

Of course, being who I really am has sometimes brought its batch of nuisance and difficult situations. I am going to tell you one of those, which was particularly grueling. But no matter what, they can try anything they want, they will not control me.

In the evening, Olivier came and met me in my quarters. He asked me if we could go out for a stroll, which I was very pleased to do. We decided to go back to our favorite spot, out of sight and out of hearing. We had put our tracksuits on to go a little more unnoticed. A beautiful night was falling. The sky was clear and sprinkled with stars. As I expected, Olivier asked me a few more questions on alien life and shadow leaders. I was telling him what I knew when suddenly, I felt a ship coming in the sky. I pointed it to Olivier. It was coming at high speed from the northwest. It was oval shaped and entirely surrounded by a blazing white light. The next minute, it flew over us and dove into the ocean, right in front of us.

I heard Olivier say "Wow" several times. Then after a few minutes, he said: "Good heavens! It was incredible! This is the first time in my life I have seen this. And it is the first time I've seen one so close."

"I must admit I did not expect it to dive into the sea before us," I answered.

Olivier, who was still stunned, did not say a word. We stayed there a few long minutes watching toward the spot where the craft had disappeared.

Then, out of the blue, a coast guard vehicle burst into view at full speed. I had time to tell Olivier not to speak, that I would do the talking. The cops, five or six of them, ran toward us.

"Stand still and put your hands above your heads," one of them yelled.

The situation was getting more complicated. I wondered how we were going to get ourselves out of that mess.

Olivier looked at me, uneasy, with a hint of panic in his eyes.

"Keep calm," I whispered to him. "Everything is going to be fine."

I was trying to convince myself as well because, quite frankly, I was anxious too.

"Names and ID numbers," one of the policemen asked.

Meanwhile, another one searched us. They found my pack of cigarettes and my lighter, as well as my military card and my keys. Nothing else. Olivier did not have anything on him apart from his keys.

"What were you doing here? You know this is a forbidden area?"

"We were jogging and then, after one hour or so, we stopped here to sit down and have a chat. We didn't know it was a forbidden area. Where is it posted?"

"Do you want us to believe you were exercising? At this time of the day? Isn't the base big enough for you to practice?"

"But that's the truth of it. We were running to unwind. We love going out in the evening when it's cool and watching the ocean."

"Don't bullshit me. I'm asking you this once again. What the hell were you doing here?"

"But we're telling you we were exercising, only exercising. What's going on? What do you have against us?"

Olivier was starting to lose patience.

"Yes, damn it! What's wrong with jogging in the evening?"

"Watch out! Don't get clever with me! I'm the one asking questions here."

"Sir, I think they are telling the truth. Besides, we haven't found anything on them," another policeman told his superior.

"OK then! But I don't want to see you around here anymore! Is that understood? Or else, you'll be in serious trouble."

"Yes, sir!"

"Go on then! Back to your quarters. I don't want to see you again."

And off we ran. Phew! That was a close call.

An Unexpected Event

After we went back to the base and took our showers, Olivier wanted us to meet up and talk about what had just happened. I suggested we meet by the trees behind our building, and above all, keep a low profile. I could feel something was about to happen.

I had barely opened the door to get out when I came face to face with an officer in the corridor.

"What are you doing?" he asked me.

"Evening, sir. I'm going out for a smoke because I can't get to sleep."

"Ah! Fine. Don't hang around outside and try and get some sleep."

"Right, sir."

"Good night."

"Thanks. Good night to you too."

Once I was outside, I had time to have a smoke before Olivier arrived.

"We have to hurry. I've just bumped into an officer on my way out. And he looked at me suspiciously," I told him to get him into the swing.

"OK," he replied. "In this case, I'm not going to beat around the bush. Don't you find it really strange that after what we'd just seen, a patrol should show up and come down on us?"

"Indeed. These are disturbing matches and/or coincidences. It's as if they were looking for something. At the same time, they weren't really comfortable. They were tense, even more than us."

"Really? I didn't notice the difference. I wasn't comfortable at all."

"In any case, one thing is for certain: it is not a coincidence that they showed up precisely at the spot where we saw the craft disappear into the water."

"Oh! Do you think they were tracking it?"

"Yes, I'm sure they saw it just as we did."

"Wow! And do you think they wanted to know if we saw it?"

"I'm sure they did. We were right not to say anything to them. Honestly, I don't know what they would have done afterward. Besides ..."

A car was coming. We cut short our conversation and went around the back to our rooms. We did not want to take any risks anymore. After a short night, Olivier and I met in the laundry. The evening's events would obviously give us the thread of our discussion.

We were gathered together under the porch for roll call. The sergeant major called us one by one. Nobody was missing this morning. He started giving his instructions to the green space maintenance team when he was interrupted by the arrival of a vehicle. It was a coast guard minivan.

They saluted our sergeant major and asked him: "Where are Sailors Rousseau and Lenoy?"

"Here," he told them with a shaky and faltering voice. He was apparently as surprised as we were.

"Sailors Rousseau and Lenoy, put your hands behind your backs. You are taken into custody."

No one said a word. Everybody was at once surprised and transfixed by what was happening. We found ourselves handcuffed and taken away in the minivan in full view of all our colleagues and our superior. The sergeant major came toward us, puzzled and doubtful.

"May I know what is going on?" he asked us.

"I don't know any more than you do," I replied with a shrug.

Into Custody

We were taken to the coast guards which were at the entrance of the base. I must say that having my hands handcuffed behind my back while sitting in a car is uncomfortable, in every sense of the word.

Olivier glanced at me every now and then. He was disoriented and obviously worried. And rightly so. I was not doing too well either. The trip seemed to last a lifetime. We went past many people on the way. People sometimes recognized us and turned around, which ended up making us even more uncomfortable than we were. Once we arrived at the car park, they made us get out of the vehicle and grabbed our arms. Other soldiers, who were there, wondered at the sight of us being escorted by the cops.

I was starting to think that this was a bad movie and that it would stop. Once we were inside the building, our bodyguards asked us to stay in the reception area, and they each went to a different room. A few moments later, they came back and separated Olivier and me. We were each taken to an office, well away from each other. Another policeman came in and asked me to sit down.

"Excuse me, but are these really necessary?" I asked about my handcuffs.

He took them off and asked me not to try anything, such as running away.

My wrists hurt. I now understood how criminals felt when arrested.

"Surname, first names, ID number, date of birth?"

The interrogation began. My host's voice was firm and he looked tough. I suspected that it would not be a pleasant experience. Once he had checked my identity, he asked me if I had a police record. As I was sure that he had everything on the screen before him, I thought that he was testing me to see how I would react, and I told him I didn't. He also asked me if I had any problems fitting in on the base, or troubles with anyone in particular. I replied in the negative.

Tons of questions then followed. I did not know what he was getting at, but it was sometimes quite far from what I could expect. What was he trying to do? Assess me psychologically? Morally? My inner voice was telling me to beware and not fall into their traps. They want to throw me off balance? They do not know me well. I am tenacious and when needed, I can be strong-headed. Two or three hours had gone by. I sensed that the cop was starting to lose patience. He got up and asked me to stay put. He went out and slammed the door behind him. I thought of Olivier and wondered whether everything was going well for him.

"Do not worry about him. Everything is going to be fine," Ezahyel told me.

"Oh, you are here? This is good timing. You'll have to explain to me what I am doing here. What we are doing here. In my opinion, we don't belong in that place and we shouldn't be considered as thugs. What's going on?"

"Remain confident. Stay who you are. They are trying to find out some things. They will try anything to get what they want. They will even try to get you to say or admit these things. Just stick to your guns, David, and everything will go smoothly despite appearances. I insist, it is all appearances."

"Yeah, I have the feeling that it's not going to be a piece of cake."

The door had just opened again abruptly. It was a different cop. It was like a B movie, where the bad cop steps in, just to intimidate you a bit. I found it pathetic.

"So, Sailor Rousseau, what were you doing in that forbidden area of the base? Tell us and we will be more magnanimous."

"I already told your predecessor many times. It's not going to start all over again, is it?"

"We ask the questions here. So, tell me why you were at that spot. Now!"

"Oh, you can get mad. I'm not intimidated at all, you know."

"Oh yeah? That's the way you take it. You know you're up to your neck in shit, David?"

"Ah, we're on first name terms, now? No problem. I don't have any objections. But what shit are you talking about?"

"Because now you're playing dumb? Like you don't know what you've done? You want to deny it?"

"Of course I deny it. I haven't done anything. What exactly am I being blamed for? Because I don't know."

"Trying to be too clever by half! You're digging yourself in deeper, believe me. You'd be better off admitting what you did. It would greatly ease your sentence."

"Yes, sure! I don't even know about it. I don't even know what you're talking about. So, yes, of course, I'm going to confess to a crime I didn't commit."

"Ah! So, you do confess to a crime?"

"But oh! Are you crazy? I'm telling you I haven't done anything. What are you accusing me of?"

"You know very well. Stop playing that little game of yours."

"No, I do not know. You, on the other hand, are playing a game. And I am not going to play it."

He slammed his fist on the table. His eyes got dark.

"Very well! No more jokes!" he yelled and left the room.

Now I think I'm in serious trouble. I don't know what they really want, but they are anxious to make us confess to something we haven't done. It's been going on for several hours now. We haven't eaten anything. It must be around two in the afternoon. Besides, I'm thirsty. I have to ask them for water. It's not normal that we are not given anything. They can't do that.

The door opened again and yet a different cop entered the room. It was the third policeman to come to interrogate me. How long was their nonsense going to last?

"Before we start anything, I'd like you to bring me some water. I'm very thirsty. You can't keep us like this without giving us anything. We have rights. We are not beasts," I told him firmly.

"You are right. Please excuse my colleagues for this oversight," he replied.

A few moments later, he was back with some water, something to nibble on, and a cup of coffee.

"Right, let's start from the beginning," he said as I ate and drank.

"I don't believe it! Is this a joke?"

"A joke? Do I look like I am joking around?" he asked me seriously.

And it was the same tune again. He interrogated me for at least a good two hours but gained nothing more than his predecessors. Unlike the others, this cop remained calm. Too calm perhaps.

"So, if I am to sum up what you said, you were there only because you were exercising? At nightfall? In a forbidden area?" he resumed.

"Yes! That's what I keep telling you. When are you going to stop your stupid interrogation?" This time, I was the one starting to lose patience.

"Ah! You want to get angry? In here? Go for it, then! Be my guest!"

I did not have time to reply.

"So, you are denying the facts? Is that it?"

"The facts? Dammit! What facts are you talking about?"

"All the sensitive military equipment which disappeared from the warehouse on the infamous night we found you on the waste ground."

"How convenient! And I suppose we stole it? You accuse us of theft when we have committed no crime? Do you have any evidence? Because it is getting more serious than I thought."

"Our investigators are still looking for the evidence. They're searching your quarters and questioning the witnesses at this very moment."

"Witnesses? What witnesses?"

"I'm the one asking the questions here!"

"Yes, and don't we have the right to defend ourselves?'"

"Defend yourselves? Do you want to call a lawyer?"

"I do, if it goes on like this."

"Do you have one?"

"Of course I do."

"Have you ever needed his services? Have you dealt with the law in the past?"

"No, I haven't. And I hope I never will. But it's best to be careful. Besides, he is not just any lawyer."

"What's his name?"

"You'll know if I have to get in touch with him."

This time around, the cop remained quiet and looked disconcerted. He got up and walked out.

CHAPTER VII

Military Secrets

We were held in custody until late at night. They had brought us a meal tray for dinner. I had taken advantage of that break to think and rethink the day's events, given they had left me alone to eat. I had no news of Olivier. I did not know whether he was still there or if he had cracked. I hoped he was strong enough to cope. In situations like this, anyone could blow a fuse and say things involuntarily under pressure or stress. Or even confess things that are not true but which are confessed out of fear or for fear of reprisal, in order to be left alone.

Without giving us much respite, the interrogation started again half an hour after our culinary break. And that time, it was not one or two but three policemen calling the tune. Their boss, the sergeant major, was there. He was a tall, well-built man in his forties with a harsh, expressionless face and a deeply wrinkled forehead. He started interrogating me in turn. And for the umpteenth time, I had to repeat my account and defend myself against their accusations.

"Stealing sensitive military equipment is considered an act of treason, you know. Plainly, the consequences will be huge. You may be sent to jail for many years. Military courts are not as lenient as a civilian court. You are heading for serious troubles which will tarnish your life for a long time, believe me."

"But I'm telling you we are innocent, dammit! How do I have to explain it to you? We've done nothing wrong. Absolutely nothing."

"You want me to believe you're innocent?" He started laughing.

"Absolutely! I have a clear conscience. What about you?"

"Don't mess with me! You don't seem to understand the

seriousness of your acts and of you denying them."

"I'm not messing with you. I'm just telling you the truth. But none of you seems willing to take it into account. I think all this custody and interrogation is just a sham."

The sergeant major got up and his chair fell backward. He went around the table and grabbed me by my collar.

I did not have time to dodge him. He lifted me from my chair and pinned me against the wall, threatening me: "Right, now you're going to tell me the truth!"

"Oh … oh … calm down! You have to stop watching westerns and whodunnits on TV. You're not Clint Eastwood!" I said.

One of the other cops started snorting.

"Tell me the truth or it will end very badly for you!"

"All right! You want the truth, mate? I'll tell you the truth! But first let me go."

Without realizing it, I had started talking to him very casually. He seemed to take no notice.

"Careful! No trick!" he warned me.

"So, here it is. The reason Olivier and I were over there was because we saw an unidentified flying object, which then disappeared into the ocean. And that's when one of your patrols bumped into us. There you go, you know it all, now."

"A UFO? You want to convince me you saw a UFO?"

"We did! Not only did we see it, but I can also confirm it."

The three of them started chatting at the back of the room, so that I could not hear what they were saying. After a couple of minutes, the sergeant major came back to me and told me: "You are going to spend the night in a cell. It will make you think about your future."

A Night in Jail

When I was taken behind bars, I thought that this was it, I was up to my neck in trouble. The feeling one has is indescribable. The little freedom one has left is blown away with the last glimmers of hope. How can a human being be caged in such a way that he loses all his bearings, his dignity, and his sovereignty? I could understand and feel what a prisoner went through, because I was going through it too. It must have come from my empathy too. No matter the situation, I can easily feel what people who have experienced the same thing feel. Empathy is a very good thing, but it has to be mastered. In the sense that you must not let yourself be impregnated, otherwise it would soon consume you. Take everything with detachment. Don't keep anything. This is what I have learned over the years and from all these experiences. I tried to look in the hallway through the small window in my cell door, in order to find Olivier. But I saw nothing.

In front of me was a wall. The other cells must have been a little farther away. I hope he's OK and that he's holding up. Oh God, please let him be OK.

"Do you remember what I told you earlier, David?"

"Ezahyel, I'm relieved to hear you. You can't imagine how relieved I am. We tend to think we are all alone in such moments."

"You are never alone. Have you already forgotten that?"

"No, I haven't! Of course not. It's just that it is very hard. I wouldn't wish it on anyone. I honestly wouldn't."

"Yes. And that is why we are always here. Not everyone is aware of it. But we are always here."

"You protect us, like guardian angels ..."

"So to speak. Your religions, your dogmas, your beliefs call us many names."

"What about Olivier? Does someone always keep watch over him too, then?"

"Oh, yes. And there are several of them."

"How is he doing?"

"He also got carried away at times, just like you. But on the whole, he is fine. He too has understood your policemen's scheme."

"Ah, very good. I knew it, deep down. It takes more to destabilize him."

"Yes, that is right."

"Tell me, Ezahyel, how much longer do we have to endure this?"

"It is almost over. They will release you shortly."

"Ah, thanks. I'm so happy to hear you say this."

"You should expect something else."

"Like what?"

"Do you think that they are going to leave you like this without doing anything, after what you have told them?"

"Er … I suppose not. What's your point? You're starting to worry me."

"Do not worry. We protect you."

"Ezahyel, wait …"

"I am being called away, David. I will be back as soon as possible. Try and get some sleep. You need to regenerate."

"Sleep? How could I possibly sleep with all that's happened?"

"Welcome and accept …" he told me in a distant voice.

Still, Ezahyel must have eased my mind, because I slept for a few hours anyway. I was awakened at dawn by a guard bringing me breakfast.

"What time is it?" I asked him.

"It's six o'clock. After your breakfast, I will take you to our health section, where you can have a shower. At eight o'clock, you are expected, so be ready."

"Expected? By whom?"

"Our sergeant major will answer you."

"May I at least give a call to my lawyer to inform him?"

"No, you can't."

"I can't?"

"That won't be necessary."

"I beg your pardon?"

"I can't tell you more."

"Please excuse me, but I don't trust you."

"And we understand that. That's normal."

"We? Who's we?"

"I can't tell you anything."

"Either you have told me too much already or …"

"Be sure of one thing. You are not alone."

Those words resonated with me and deep down, something or someone told me I could trust them.

"OK! All right then. Anyway, I have nothing to lose at this point."

"In this case, get ready and leave it to us."

He left, leaving me in suspense. The longer it went on, the more bizarre things occurred. What exactly was going on? Some points would need to be clarified. But first, I needed to get out of here. Once I had showered, I was escorted to the reception.

What a surprise to find out that Olivier was already there. I smiled broadly at him so that he would understand that everything was fine for me and to see his reaction. He smiled back at me. But he looked exhausted, weary. I was made to sit next to him. The policeman took some handcuffs out. Another cop told him it would not be necessary.

"How are you, Olivier?" I asked him in a whisper.

"I'm OK. Tired and frazzled, but I'm OK. What about you?"

"Just the same as you, I'd say. The guys have really put us through the wringer."

"Yeah! Tell me about it! By the end, I just couldn't take it anymore. It was never-ending. They also told me that you confessed everything. Is that true?"

"What did they tell you?"

"Not much, except that you had finally confessed. But confessed to what? I didn't have a clue. They started accusing me of all kinds of things ... you know."

"Yes, same here. But I did not fall for their games."

"What did you tell them, then?"

"That we had seen a UFO."

"What? You told them?"

"Yes, their farce had been going on for too long. So, I told them to get us out of this mess."

"And did they believe you?"

"I don't know. All I know is that it bothered them. As a result, they told me I would spend the night in a cell."

"What now?"

"All I'm asking is that you trust me. Don't ask me why or how. I'll tell you later."

Meeting the General

We did not know what else was in store for us and we were not comfortable. Many questions were running through our minds, one after the other. I was lost in my thoughts when a policeman came toward us.

"Sailors Rousseau and Lenoy, please follow me."

He made us get into a minivan. Our driver remained quiet

and it was getting too oppressive.

"May we ask where you are taking us?" I asked him.

"You are being summoned by the base general. He's waiting for you in his office."

"The general?"

"Yes, absolutely."

We both started feeling bad. What was going to happen to us now? I could see the confusion in Olivier's eyes.

Would it ever end?

"Don't be afraid. Everything is going to be fine," our driver said to us while looking at us in his rear-view mirror.

"How can you tell?" I retorted.

"You are not alone."

"What does it mean? You're the second person to tell me that this morning. Who exactly are you? And what are those mysteries about?"

"Stay confident and above all, be honest with the general. I'll take you to the door of his office, then everything will be in your hands. By the way, we never had this conversation."

"What? What do you mean?"

"I didn't tell you anything. Did you hear me say anything?"

"Er, no, I didn't," I stammered.

He winked at us in the rear-view mirror. When we got there, he escorted us to the general. On our way there, we encountered many officers, whom we had to salute as we went by. I must say that the pressure was starting to rise. I was getting more and more nervous. When our guide signaled us to wait behind him and knocked on the door, it added to our anxiety.

"Come in!" a loud voice replied behind the door.

"General! I'm bringing you Sailors Rousseau and Lenoy at your command."

"Very good, captain. Bring them in and close the door behind you."

"Yes, sir."

"At ease, sailors! So, Mister Rousseau and Mister Lenoy, tell me what is happening to you."

As I preferred to move forward unwaveringly and determinedly, I took action and replied: "This is a terrible misunderstanding, sir."

"Is this? Please clarify and be honest. I was not born

yesterday."

"You want me to be honest? Very good, I shall be honest, as I have always been. The night before yesterday, while we were out for a walk after a jog with Olivier, we saw an unidentified flying object. We didn't let it out of our sight until it disappeared into the ocean. And then, a coast guard patrol came upon us. Following this, they came to arrest us the next morning and remanded us in custody. This is what happened. Truthfully."

"You're saying you observed a UFO? Is that right? And what do you think it was? What did it look like?"

"Well, it's a little hard to describe it, sir. It was oval in shape and gave off an intense bluish-white glow that surrounded it completely. We didn't see what it really looked like," Olivier answered.

"Ah, so you do not know what it was?"

"No! But all I can say is that it was of nonhuman origin," I added.

"Was it now? And what makes you say this, Mr. Rousseau?"

"It made no sound. There was no release of fossil material either. It flew over us without making the slightest noise and then dived into the ocean. What kind of terrestrial aircraft could do that?"

"A satellite!"

"With all due respect, sir ... a satellite?"

"Absolutely! You saw a satellite fall from space."

"But, sir ... I ..."

"You saw a satellite. Have I made myself clear? I heard you were very good sailors, Mr. Rousseau and Mr. Lenoy. Always ready to help out. If you do not want your stay among us to end badly or if you do not want to land in jail, I strongly advise you to follow my recommendations. If anyone asks you what you saw, you will reply that it was a satellite. Do I make myself clear?"

"In short, you are asking us to lie?"

"I am not! Since I told you that you saw a satellite fall, you will say that too. Unless you want to have more trouble than you do now? Think again. You won't have another opportunity like this."

The exit door was clearly looming before us. But why didn't he want us to tell the truth? And why didn't he want us to disclose the case? He must have known something. But given his rank, he simply could not talk about matters that were classified as confidential, or Top Secret, especially to us mere conscripts.

Olivier and I agreed and we accepted the deal.

"Very good, sir. If we agree, will you drop the charges against us? Because I would like to point out to you that we are still accused of stealing military equipment. Also, will you make the file disappear from your database?"

"That goes without saying. A deal is a deal. Here, look at this: it's your paper file issued by the coast guards. You see, these are your names, right?"

"Yes, indeed," I replied.

"I put it in the shredder and I will erase the digital file. No more talk of this?"

"No more talk of this, sir."

"Very good. You are smart and wise. Especially you, Mr. Rousseau. I know things about you. Be careful where you set foot. It could become very dangerous for you."

"Dangerous? What do you mean, sir?"

"I can't tell you anything more but to be careful."

"I understand, sir. Thank you, sir."

"Oh, yes, finally, if anyone asks you anything ..."

"Yes, sir. We saw a satellite fall from space."

"Very well. Now, don't let me see you again. That's an order. Dismissed, gentlemen."

"Yes, sir. Thank you, sir."

The Following Days

I might as well tell you that the following days were hard and difficult to go through. Coming back to "normality" after what we had just endured was not an easy thing to do. We also had to answer a lot of questions from our colleagues and our superiors. We were tired of having to talk things over. So much so that on the second day, I couldn't help but tell the truth to those who had ears to hear. Olivier was reassured not at all.

"Have you forgotten our agreement with the general?" he shouted out.

"No, I haven't forgotten. But what do you expect them to do

to us? We've been asked to keep quiet so that the case does not get out and the media doesn't pick up the story. The army knows a lot of things. They have their secrets. If we were to keep quiet, they would manipulate us at will with threats or whatever. And I disagree with this. They cannot prevent us from being free. By acting in this way, they stay in control, see? On the other hand, when information goes around and/or things are disclosed, they lose control and that way, it is completely out of their hands. They can only deny the facts. By saying things, we are protected ... to a certain extent."

"It doesn't exactly fill me with confidence!"

"Don't worry, Olivier. Everything will be fine. Besides, I don't intend to stop here."

"Huh? What are you going to do now?"

"Well, I'm going to write an article and send it to one or two specialized magazines."

"And you think it is going to protect you? Protect us?"

"In some way, yes."

"Are you going to mention my name?"

"Only if you agree."

"No, I don't. I'd rather you didn't. There are too many risks involved. It could fall on my family."

"It's true that there is a risk of it affecting our family members. Don't worry, I'll use pseudonyms."

"And when do you plan to do this?"

"This weekend. As I'm going home, I might as well write everything down while it's still fresh and send it to the recipients right away. But I don't know how I'm going to tell my parents, though."

"Yeah, same for me ... I think I won't tell them anything. My dad might make a scene and turn up here."

"In any case, everyone we talked to on the base took us seriously and they were very surprised at how big it had become."

Some of them even started calling me Mulder,[12] and I must admit that I liked that. This American series, which had just been released in France, dealt with all the subjects that fascinate me.

---

12   Mulder is a fictional character from The X-Files series, which was broadcast by M6, a French TV channel, in June 1994. It was based on real facts and dealt with top-secret cases, unsolved cases such as paranormal phenomena and other alien abductions.

And I thought it was an excellent way of getting people used to this other, unexplained thing. I thought disclosure through TV was very clever. It started a long time ago, by the way. Many series and movies are actually about disclosure. Where some people only see sci-fi, I see a kind of documentary. It all depends on our point of view.

A Mysterious Disappearance

One thing was for certain, more and more odd things were happening on the base. I heard that an elite commando had been found dead in the base harbor. Cause of death: drowning. The most surprising thing is that they are supposed to be over-trained and used to diving and swimming. So what exactly had happened? Also, was it a coincidence that it happened only a few days after we spotted the craft and were arrested? This was quite a lot in such a short time. Not to mention all the top brass who had shown up since the morning. There were generals, admirals, majors, etc. And they all looked tense, nervous. I could see it in the energy of those I met. Some were running around. It must have been of the utmost importance. If only I could see the captain who took us to the general's office again, he must know something for sure.

On my way back to the laundry room after my truck driving course, I bumped into my sergeant. I took the opportunity to call out to him:

"Sir! Do you have a minute, please?"

"Yes. What is it?"

"I wanted to ask you … Do you know what's been going on here today?"

"Absolutely not! I have no idea what all these officers are doing here. I wasn't even notified of their arrival, nor invited to any meeting of any kind."

"It's quite strange, don't you think?"

"Mr. Rousseau, if I were you, I would remain discreet. Especially after what has just happened. Even if all charges have been dropped against you, I'd keep a low profile if I were you. Don't forget where you are."

"Of course, I'm aware of that. Would you doubt me, sir?"

"No, I wouldn't. I know you're honest, and I know you're a good guy. But don't look where you shouldn't. Take my word for it. It will be better for you."

"Sir, you do admit there are some unusual things happening on this base?"

"Look, there's always been some weird stuff going on here. This is a field marine base, and it's also an arsenal. They build ships and submarines here. Maybe even nuclear energy, who knows. It's better to avoid sticking your nose everywhere anyway."

"If you don't mind me saying so, I think they even use technologies that aren't supposed to exist."

"How's that?"

"I'm sorry, but I'd rather keep this to myself. I don't want to put you in a bad position."

"Indeed! On second thought, it suits me just fine. I'm not far from retirement now."

"How much time do you have left?"

"Two years. Two years to go and it's demob."

"I understand, sir. I won't bother you with my questions anymore."

"Thanks."

"No, thank you, sir."

The day was over and all was quiet on the base again. It seemed that the top brass had left. However, no one knew why they suddenly came. Olivier had decided to go home every night from now on, in order to take a step back from all this. I could understand it.

After dinner, I too decided to have some peace and quiet and I went back to my quarters to read a good book. I opened my closet after removing the lock, and there, to my great surprise, I found two books. They were about sixty pages each and written by a man named Milton William Cooper. They were entitled: Majestic 12 and the Secret Government and Operation Trojan Horse.

How could these books end up in my closet? My lock was on it and had not been forced or cut. So how? And who? Who could have done this? And without leaving a trace, besides. I was alone in the room as the guys were still outside, so I took the opportunity to lie down on my bed and look through these mysterious manuscripts that had come there by some miracle or magic. Another riddle that I had to solve.

From the very first pages, the tone was set. It was all about MJ12, its secrets, and the alien presence on Earth.

Many things confirmed what I knew about the shadow government. But I learned some other things that came as a surprise. I was still far from having imagined all their schemes. The question was: to what extent did they control events?

Olivier would be surprised the next day when I told him what happened when I opened my closet. We now had to find out who had put the books there. It was clear that someone was keeping up closely with what I was doing outside the base. And that person, to my mind, was well placed ...

"Indeed, my brother."

"Ezahyel! I'm thrilled to hear you again. Can you tell me more?"

"Let's say you have found an ally. And a good one at that."

"Really? But who is he?"

"His identity will remain hidden from you. But he is ready to act in confidence."

"But how? I don't understand! What exactly is it about? Can you tell me more without giving me his name?"

"Let's say he works for a group whose goal is to free the Earth. Individuals from this group have infiltrated all sectors to overthrow the power from within and bring to light what is in the shadows, while others are waiting for the right time to take action."

"Wow, that's great! Is it possible to join this group? I would love to be a member and participate in this operation."

"But you already are."

"What? What do you mean, I already am?"

"Yes, brother. It's still a little early to tell you, but you are an integral part of this operation. Not in the same group, but in a different one."

"Now you're losing me. How many groups are there in total?"

"Two of them."

"Two?"

"That's right. An alliance was made between humans and beings from various universes, including your original creators."

The Alliance

"That's awesome. I'm so happy to hear that. And what group do I belong to, then?"

"The galactic alliance."

"The galactic alliance? Wow! I knew it in my heart."

"Of course you did."

"And what about the other group? What is it called?"

"The Earth alliance."

"It's so simple and yet so meaningful."

"Yes, that is right."

"But then, what am I supposed to be doing in this alliance?"

"You will remember in due time."

"So, if I sum it up, someone on this base is part of the Earth alliance, and he's helping me out, right?"

"That is one way of putting it, yes."

"And does he know I'm part of the galactic alliance?"

"Yes, he does."

"But how? It's a little bit beyond me ..."

"You'll understand a lot better when you remember."

"So, this alliance guy here put these books in my closet?"

"That is right."

"But for what purpose exactly?"

"To guide you on your path."

"My path?"

"The one that will lead you back to who you really are, yes."

"Wow! Thank you, Ezahyel! Thank you all! Oh, but wait ... My ally is the captain, right?"

I didn't get an answer. Ezahyel's silence meant more than words. But would I ever see him again? That was the question.

Allies for the Liberation

The next morning, I waited for Olivier with some excitement. It was Friday and I was going home at midday for the weekend. Olivier arrived just before the call. I was able to tell him discreetly that I had to talk to him.

"Has something happened again?" he asked me.

"Oh, yes! I'll explain later."

Once the call was over and the mission orders were given, the sergeant major asked me to come and see him in his office.

"What's going on, sir?"

"You're taking your driving test next week, aren't you?"

"Yes, that's right, sir!"

"Very good, because I'm going to need you as soon as possible. Our current driver finishes his military service next week. From Monday on, you will no longer be working in the laundry. You will stay with the response team to get familiar with the equipment and the naval firefighters."

"Yes, sir!"

"You will receive all your gear on Monday morning. Training will begin at ten. Any questions?"

"No, sir!"

"Very well, then. You may leave. Have a good weekend!"

"Thank you, sir! You, too, sir."

On my way out, I went straight to Olivier to tell him about these changes. He was a little disappointed to learn that I would no longer be with him all day, working and sharing all those moments. I felt the same. Still, he was surprised by what I told him about the books that appeared in my closet and the conversation I had had with Ezahyel.

"But who put these books in your closet?"

"I'm not sure yet, even if I have an idea."

"Anyway, it's clear that they want to lead you to a particular track or aspect."

"Yes, that's right. And it's around those who run this world in the shadows. There's no doubt about it."

"Maybe we should take some precautions, don't you think? Are you still planning to publish your article?"

"Yes, I do! Definitely!"

"Ah, I don't know. I have a bad feeling about this."

"Don't worry, Olivier. Don't forget that we are protected."

"We are, but to what extent?"

"I must admit that I don't know. But I am confident."

Once Olivier was reassured, I promised him that once I had read these books this weekend, I would lend them to him so that he could read them too. The end of the morning had come, and after saying good-bye to him, I headed toward the entrance to the base to get my car from the car park outside. As conscripts, we were not allowed to bring our vehicles inside. Once the key was in the ignition, I started the car and drove off, thinking about whether or not to tell my parents about what I had experienced in the last few days. How would they react if I told them?

"Don't tell them for now. It would but worry them," Ezahyel advised.

"OK! Thanks, Ezahyel."

After leaving the city center of Lorient, I turned up the music in the car during the whole journey, just to clear my head and sing to expel the emotional overload.

Back Home

When I arrived home, after a good two-hour drive, my parents greeted me and asked me how the last few weeks had gone. I told them about everything except the incident that had landed me in custody. No need to worry them too much, as I had to take my HGV driving test and then go to the army's summer camp center. That evening, after dinner, I went to my room to start writing my article.

After an hour or so, I started falling asleep. At least, my body told me that it needed to rest and recharge. When I lay down, something happened which I didn't expect at all.

Everything started to swirl. A kind of light spiral came to cover me and I was caught up in it at very high speed. I didn't have time to think as I found myself on board a ship in just a few seconds. Ezahyel was there, accompanied by three other beings, two males and one female. We can't say men and women as they are not human. Even if there are similarities in their humanoid appearance, they are not made like humans, be it from a biological or energetic point of view. Moreover, their energy is very high. A regular human being could not handle such a vibration or frequency if he is not prepared for it. What they give out in terms of radiance is just huge.

"Wow! Wow!" I said, looking around. Ezahyel and his

companions were smiling broadly.

"Indeed, David, we have brought you up to our ship because there are several things we need to talk to you about."

"This is fantastic! Amazing. I've never been back here since the first time[13] you brought me on board. But it feels a bit like home, as if there's a part of me on this ship."

Without telling them or asking them, I walked over to an interface and began to touch it with my fingers. Functions appeared on the translucent screen. Then, out loud, I instinctively asked the onboard computer to show me my home planet in the Pleiades, as I had done the previous time. Images flashed before my eyes, like a movie. I saw myself as a child, with pale blue skin, playing with other children in plains of shimmery colors, where bright pastel blues and greens blended and waved in the gentle breeze.

Two suns were setting on the horizon, also in bluish tones. Tears rolled down my cheeks. It was so beautiful, so full of tranquility. Only one word came to mind: harmony.

Ezahyel came closer to me and started to speak: "My brother, all these memories are also inside you, in your heart. You know now that nothing is separate. Nothing separates us. You only have to remember and access your knowledge and experiences in the different life spheres."

"Yes, I know. Yet it's also so nice to do things intuitively. Because I recognize and know these devices and technologies deep down. It enables me to reconnect."

"That's right indeed," Ezahyel confirmed.

"I miss Alcyona ..."

"I understand. But remember that our planet is part of you and that you are part of it. We are one in this whole. Feel this link again, this connection."

As I refocused and directed my mind, my consciousness, to Alcyona, I could actually go back to that other time in space-time when I lived in that world. Everything was so wonderful. A telepathic link connected us all, our environment included. We were connected to this whole and we could perceive the fluctuations in the energies. And this whole vibrated at a very high frequency already. There are simply no words in human

13   This will be explained further in Book 2, as there are too many things to recount in one single volume.

language to describe this, the beauty of this harmony in this Great Whole being both so powerful and wonderful, gentle and colossal. I could also hear Alcyona's pulse, beating like a drum, in a calm and serene way. It resonated within me like a shamanic rhythm. With each pulse, you could feel waves of love spreading all over the surface. And these waves caressed you like a light summer breeze, both soft and warm. I was in perfect symbiosis with Alcyona and everything that lived there. Tears began to flow down my cheeks again.

"When will the Earth know this, Ezahyel?"

"Not right away, my brother. But don't worry. That time will come. Gaia will also ascend to higher dimensions. She has actually begun to prepare for it."

"I would so much love humans to understand and feel how splendid the wave of life is, how the One seed[14] is something both unique and universal."

"This time will come, my brother. This time will come. It cannot be otherwise."

To move on, as it were, Ezahyel said to me: "We wanted to talk to you about something. That's why we brought you on board."

From the intonation of his voice, which resonated within me, I knew that it must be important.

"What's going on, Ezahyel?"

"You have known what is happening on Mars and on the Moon since we took you there?"[15]

"Yes! I remember it very well. Why?"

"We are going to take you back to Mars. Someone asked for you."

"Huh? What do you mean, someone asked for me? I don't know anyone on Mars!"

"Think again, brother."

"But who? Why?"

"We will let the being concerned answer you."

At the same time, I felt the ship lurch to the left and head for Mars. I could see the Earth speeding away, so much so that after a few seconds it disappeared from my field of vision. The stars were

14   It contains all the frequencies of Source's original love and is in each one of us.

15   This too will be explained in Book 2.

passing by at head-spinning speed. We could see three hundred and sixty degrees thanks to technologies I cannot explain in exact terms, which allowed the ship to become completely translucent, as if the metal or alloy became crystalline by some biomechanical or chemical process. It is very impressive. Even for me, who is not a first-timer. It's always a grandiose sight.

The ship announced that we were approaching our destination. It had taken us only a few minutes to cover the distance between Earth and Mars. Incredible. And what a grandiose show to be able to see the red planet like that. Words fail me to describe what it feels like. It is not as red as it is made out to be, in fact. Not as red as you can see on NASA pictures. So where did they take these pictures? I don't really know. It doesn't match what I can see of it anyway.

Ezahyel told me that they were now going to "cloak" the ship, so as not to be seen during the descent and landing.

Because there is life on Mars. And it's not what you might expect. "Are you sure they won't see us, Ezahyel?"

"Absolutely. Don't worry."

The ship had started its descent faster than I had thought or expected. We flew over rocky massifs. In the distance—toward the east, according to Ezahyel—we could see a huge pyramid rising in the Martian sky, which was actually white, with a red-orange tinge. The pyramid was just colossal.

"Ezahyel, you'll have to tell me about this one of these days."

"Of course I will. That time will come too."

We approached what appeared to be mountains. The ship rotated counterclockwise, as if to slow down, and it positioned itself above the ground in a sort of cavity, very gently and out of sight. We had all put on a kind of one-piece suit that fit each of our body shapes. What was incredible was the fact that it was so light and yet so hardy, as strong as a dragon's shell. You could almost say that it was a second skin, as you forgot that you were wearing it so quickly and as it felt so comfortable. It automatically regulated the temperature to keep my body warm. It is true that it is cold on Mars. Very cold even at that time, about -160°F according to the ship's readings. Apparently, it could even go below 320°F. This is due to the atmosphere having lost its natural protection, like our ozone layer on Earth, Ezahyel had explained to me.

When the airlock opened under our feet, our suit began to make a slight sound and a kind of mask came to cover our face. It was almost invisible but it recycled air and oxygen to enable us to breathe. It was so pure, by the bye, that I had not breathed like that for a long time. We were floating in the void, carried by an energy beam that allowed us to reach the surface of the Martian soil.

Someone was waiting for us. He was wearing a kind of golden armor or suit made of a metallic alloy I didn't know. He was also wearing a helmet, made of the same alloy. But I could see that it was a male being with brown skin.

He had deep black eyes and long black hair. He greeted us with a broad smile.

"Sincere greetings to you, Xaman'Ek!"

"In Lak'ech Ala K'in, Ezahyel!"

I didn't know what was going on but I felt a shiver from head to toe. Not because of the cold, but rather because of the resonance of those words. They echoed in me, without me really knowing why.

"In Lak'ech Ala K'in, David! Nice to see you again."

"Er ... hi! Excuse me, but do I know you?"

"Oh, yes, you do!" he answered in a deep and warm voice.

"We have known each other for a long time. They did make you forget by taking you back in time. You are indeed younger than the last time I saw you."

"I'm lost. You must have me confused with someone else."

"No, no doubt about it, my dear friend," he maintained.

Although I must admit that he looked familiar, there was nothing coherent about what he had just told me.

"Let's go inside. We'll talk about it," he said, inviting me to follow him. We stood in front of a rock wall which, in a few seconds, revealed a hidden entrance.

"Wow!" I said in a startled voice.

"Have you really forgotten everything?" he asked me with a laugh.

"Sounds like it, yes. Why am I here?"

"I'm going to answer some of your questions. We won't have enough time for all the others. But first of all, I have to give you a healing."

"A healing? What kind of healing?"

"Your DNA and cellular memory were somewhat altered during your involvement in certain programs. Do you remember participating in something special without really knowing where these memories came from? Something that seems far away?"

"Yes, I do. For sometime now, I've been having dreams in which I see myself in different spaceships, on different planets, and in which I also talk with nonterrestrial beings. It seems so real."

"These are not mere dreams, David. They are memories. Snippets of memories, at least."

"Memories? So, was this real?"

"Yes, it was. It would take time to explain it to you now. But to sum it up, when you were a child and you were confronted with the Orion Greys, it led you to become involved in something else. Let's say that you were spotted by an organization that noted and listed all the abductions committed by these beings. This organization offered you to enter a program that was concealed from everyone. An offer that you accepted of your own free will.

"They trained you to use your empathic and psychic abilities to get in touch with other civilizations from every corner of the galaxy. And then, at the end of the said contract, you refused to extend it and they rejuvenated you and sent you back in time. That's when we first met."

"Wow! Wow! Wait a minute! How long was I involved in this?"

"Twenty of your earthly years."

"Twenty years? But how is that possible?"

"There are things in this universe that are far beyond human understanding. And I think you know that."

"I do. But let's start again, shall we?"

"We shall, but first of all, I need to give you the regeneration treatment."

Ezahyel had just entered the room. I stared at him, as if looking for support. He nodded and said: "You can trust him. Just relax. Everything is fine."

So I let Xaman'Ek act. He whispered a few words and a screen and an interface came up from the floor. A tool came out of the ceiling. It looked like a mechanical arm. At the end of it was a kind of needle made of a black stone. It looked like obsidian. I was asked to lie down but I saw no prop to do so, until a kind of table came out of the floor and waited for me to lean on it before it went horizontal. The material of this table was quite astonishing. It fitted perfectly to the shape of my body. The articulated arm started to move.

"Wait a second! Does it hurt? I have to say I hate needles."

"Not at all! Don't worry. This needle, as you call it, will not go into your body. We will amplify its energy and direct its ray directly into your DNA strands. Close your eyes and relax."

I was reassured. I gave in and closed my eyes. I immediately saw Alcyona and the Pleiades again. I think it came from Ezahyel, who was transmitting these images to me telepathically. To my great surprise, we did not stop at Alcyona but went a little farther to the outer edge of the Pleiades. To a planet called Maia. It was beautiful, a bluish green I had never seen on Earth. A few seconds later, we were in a dense forest, in which stood a village that blended into the scenery.

In perfect harmony with the environment.

In the distance, I could see a large Mayan-type pyramid, which was somewhat different but similar in structure. Gold seemed to cover it and at its top, it looked more like obsidian. It was sumptuous. The inhabitants in this village looked like Xaman'Ek. That's probably where he came from. The villagers seemed to be waiting for something. Then, some singing started to ring out. Although I couldn't understand what they meant, they gave me goosebumps. Then I realized that a ship of considerable size had appeared right above us. It was elongated and seemed made up of polished rock. Despite its imposing size, it floated there without making the slightest sound. This was a spectacular ship. Something emanated from it, I could feel it. But it was indescribable except for the feeling of familiarity.

Then, without understanding why or how, I found myself in my bed the next morning.

"Was this all a dream, then? No, it can't be. Was I there?" I wondered, both bemused and mystified.

"No, it was not a dream. You were there," Ezahyel told me.

"But what exactly happened? I was with you on Mars and then ..."

"We will explain it to you very soon. Don't worry. Everything went well. It's perfect. Get a little more rest. We will come back and see you tonight."

CHAPTER VIII

The Moon

The day went by rather quickly. I had written my article in duplicate to send it to two ufology periodicals. Without giving too much away, I merely explained the facts and nothing but the facts. The ball was set rolling. Once the mail was posted, we would see the results and/or the consequences.

In the evening, as I knew that Ezahyel was coming back, I told my parents I was going to read in my room to have quiet time. While waiting for that moment, I had really dived back into a book. I didn't have to wait very long, for a voice was heard. It was Xaman'Ek's.

"Are you ready?" he asked me.

"Of course I am!"

The truth is, I was super excited. To be reunited with them, to travel in a spaceship and see things most people wouldn't think of … I loved it. It was a little as if I did not live on Earth, yet I still lived my old life. The beam of light appeared, and everything began to swirl again. The next minute, I was inside the ship. Surprisingly enough, only Ezahyel and Xaman'Ek were on board.

"Where are the others?" I asked.

"Maira, Jehsa, and Ptesa are operating in the Aldebaran system."

"Oh, good. What about us, where are we going?"

"Fairly close by. We're going to fly over your moon."

"The Moon? But it's a dead rock! There's nothing to see on the Moon!" I said with some disappointment.

"On the contrary. There is a lot more going on there than meets the eye. Who told you it was a dead rock?"

"I don't really know. It was at school probably and from scientists on TV too. Anyway, what's out there?"

"Well, just wait a bit and you will see for yourself."

After a very short time, we arrived above the Moon. I have to say that seeing it up close is very pleasant too. What leapt out at me was its surface. It was made of a greyish earth or sand. There were a few craters, but nothing surprising there. There were a few hilly areas but again, nothing extravagant. It seemed inert, without any movement or life.

"Don't be fooled by appearances," Ezahyel announced.

"I'm sure that if you are bringing me here, there's got to be a reason."

"We've been cloaking our ship since we left the Earth's environment. And in just a few moments, we will be flying over the side of the Moon that is hidden from view on your planet."

"I have a question."

"Let's hear it."

"Did Neil Armstrong really set foot here?"

"Actually, yes and no," Xaman'Ek answered.

"What do you mean, yes and no?"

"They—the Apollo 11 crew—did come here, but they did not have time to land."

"How so? I don't understand. What happened to them?"

"Well, they got a little too close to what you're about to find out in a few moments. They had no choice but to turn back. Here we are."

"We'll wait here in a hover until the shuttle arrives," Ezahyel announced.

"The shuttle? What shuttle?"

"Be patient, my brother."

"Here it is," Xaman'Ek announced.

I could see a dot moving and approaching rapidly from the southeast. The object passed us by without spotting us. It was not very big. The size of a car I would say, the size of a sedan but a little taller. It circled twice over an open area, and suddenly, some kind of halogen lights began to illuminate the landing area. A few seconds later, a huge trapdoor opened on the lunar ground. The illusion was perfect. I had seen nothing earlier. The shuttle rushed in, with three human passengers on board according to what Ezahyel had disclosed. Our ship moved as well to come over this unsuspected opening in the lunar soil. And there, I was astounded and dumbstruck to see what was inside. There was a whole facility, made of metal, with a spaceship parking area in its center. There were ships of all sizes. Some were triangular in shape, others were much larger and looked oddly like the Imperial ships in Star Wars, except that they were darker. I had time to make out some movements below. Some men in suits were busy, but not just them. I could also make out much taller nonhuman beings with tails. It was incredible. Stunning even.

"But what is going on here? Who are these men? And in particular, who are these beings?"

"They are of reptilian origin and they come from the Orion star system. The men you saw collaborate with them. They've been here since your second world war."

"Since World War II? You've got to be kidding me. What's all this about?"

"You need to understand something, David. Space programs have been around a lot longer than you've been told on Earth. They have been especially on the increase since the beginning of your twentieth century, when Eastern European men allied themselves with involutionary entities. Reverse engineering technologies were developed, as well as technologies made from information outside your world. The Germans were able to build their first antigravity ships for space travel. They were able to go to the Moon and take over the place. A place that had existed for a long time, in fact. You should know that your Moon is not a natural satellite, by the way. It was put there a long time ago by a nation from another star system. But we will talk about that later. In any case, the Germans tried to keep it all very secret, because they were so technologically advanced compared to other countries in your world. But there were leaks. The Americans—among others—had infiltrated the German programs. Before the end of the Second World War, all the people who were working on these advanced technologies were expatriated to Antarctica with the fruit of their labors. In Antarctica, there is a facility from a very ancient civilization and it is located beneath the ice. But I will tell you more about that later. So, the Germans continued their program in the utmost secrecy, nowhere near the war. The Black Fleet was born. With the collaboration of the reptilian beings, they made interplanetary journeys. They went to the Aldebaran system, among other places. They did not hesitate to use force. Several worlds have since disappeared. Others have fallen into slavery. Humans are used as commodities to be bartered. Their thirst for power and domination is ever increasing."

Other space programs have been developed simultaneously and secretly in several countries. Some alliances were formed with nations from the Galactic Federation to counteract the plans and actions of the Black Fleet. And ..."

"Hold on, hold on ... I'm sorry, Xaman'Ek, but that's way too much information to take in at once. It's crazy and huge at the same time. On the one hand, I find it hard to believe, and on the other, I'm not surprised. How is it that all this seems real to me, when it's inconceivable all the same? For a regular human, I mean. Many people get locked up for less. Do you realize the impact?"

"Yes, I do. And I also know that I can tell you about it because, crazy as it may seem to you, you have been part of it."

"Oh my! Now I have to sit down, I feel like I'm going to lose my marbles."

"Take some time to relax and take a deep breath," Ezahyel tells me.

"We can show you if you wish. The holographic recordings will speak louder than words," Xaman'Ek suggested. "Ah, because there are recordings too?"

"You don't have to watch them. But it's time for you to understand. Implants prevent you from remembering some things. Their function is to block and/or restrain your experiences. There are even words that you can't say because in your mind, they seem to be nonexistent," Ezahyel concluded.

My heart was starting to race. All this information was buzzing through my mind. They were going round and round in circles without stopping. I could no longer see clearly. A headache was showing its teeth, along with dizziness. I wasn't usually prone to dizzy spells but this time, I lost my footing in the meanders of incomprehension and I fell unconscious.

When I woke up, we were back on Mars. Xaman'Ek was by my side. I felt I had a hangover. But other than that, I felt much better. Emotionally speaking, I felt lighter, more serene.

"What did you do to me, Xaman'Ek?"

"I gave you a healing with crystals to soothe your scattered mind."

"Thank you very much. It's true that it was a bit too much

for my human understanding. Even though I know, deep down, that it is all real and that it explains a lot, I think it's going to take me a little while to really remember what happened. Also, if you don't mind, I'd like to remember it myself."

"Very well, I understand. It is a commendable thing to do."

"I would ask you then, if it is possible, to block this whole memory sequence in me for a while."

"It is possible to put it back to sleep, indeed."

"Great! But before that, I'd like you to tell me a little about it. When and how did it start?"

"Following your reunion with Ezahyel and the abductions conducted by the Greys, an Earth alliance military group became interested in you. Every abduction case is tracked. Thanks to the signal transmitted by the implants, they know who is abducted, when and where you are. After this, they made you an offer, which you accepted. That's how you joined them."

"Wow! So I went of my own free will?"

"Yes, you did! Let's say that, knowing who you really were, your soul made this choice of experience in order to be at the heart of the event and to bring a little light to it."

"OK! Don't tell me more for now, Xaman'Ek, will you?"

"As you wish."

"Thanks again. Can you tell me a little more about yourself? What's your story? Where do you come from?"

"This is going to take a while, so I'll just give you the outlines."

"OK. It's fine by me."

The Ancient Mayans

"I come from the ancient Mayan civilization that has been on Earth for thousands of years. We were reputed for our advances in writing, art, architecture, agriculture, mathematics, and astronomy. Contrary to what your researchers think, we were not born on Earth. We originate from the Pleiades. We were on Earth both for our own experiences and to guide man.

"Long ago, some wars broke out in the Orion star system. The reptilian beings started it. The reptilians were also very advanced, both technologically and spiritually. Many of them found enlightenment and placed themselves in the heart to truly know the breath of life from the Source. Some even succeeded in becoming one with the Great Whole. They reached the highest vibration of the fifth dimension.

"There were more and more couples among them. These beings were able to heighten their extrasensory faculties and ability to project their consciousness over a distance. The creative power of their thought reached its pinnacle. They could even enter the genetic code of the matrix and create life. That's how highly evolved they were. Some individuals could even ascend into the sixth- and seventh-dimensional vibrations, while others excelled in the fields of science, especially genetics. They doubtlessly became the greatest geneticists in our universe. As their world evolved, some of those who had gained power were parasitized by an involutionary entity that had managed to corrupt their minds and hearts, causing them to become self-centered, forcing them to turn their attention to themselves and not to others, thus creating a dissension in the balance and energy and within the federation itself.

"War broke out. Worlds and civilizations were wiped out. Shock and fear weaved their way everywhere. Using a huge ship—the size of a planet—these involutive beings spread chaos and destruction. Since their aim was to block the evolution process, they succeeded in lowering the vibrations to keep the universe in the third and fourth dimensions.

"That way, they were able to keep control and power and hold billions of souls in slavery throughout the system. Fortunately, the worlds that were in higher dimensions were able to keep their protection and the threat at bay. Yet clearly, the Federation had suffered a great blow. The Sirius Council, understanding that the involutionary beings were seeking to block the Federation in its process of raising consciousness, ordered that troops of specialized warriors be formed to deal with this terrible threat— the worst they had known so far.

"Only the ascended masters' intervention brought an end to this destructive armed conflict. But this conflict was deported, if I may say so, in order to be brought to a conclusion all the same, because it is not possible to interfere with the souls' choices and this war takes many forms even today. It takes place on one life sphere alone. For only this planet could accept and welcome it in this galactic dial."

"Let me guess ... the Earth?"

"Yes! Absolutely."

"The Orion wars resulted in the fragmentations of individuals, which created duality, so to speak. From then on, there were two sources. One was creative and loving, and the other dark and destructive. Urantia—Gaia—received this scourge to enable all these souls to remember who they really were and to make their choice. So that all these souls could recover their integrity and access the love of the higher dimensions when the time to ascend would come again. But in the meantime, healing would be weighty, so great would the emotional charge be and so deeply ingrained in the consciousnesses the trauma. It would require a huge amount of purification work. Because many turned away from the original source when they arrived on Earth in the third dimension's low density, souls made this choice and volunteered to forget everything in order to remember who they were and to transmute everything for the arrival of the next evolutionary cycle of the breath of life."

I could not hold back my tears. I felt so many things at once. I could feel the joy and love that animated all these peoples and at the same time, I understood their dismay and the trauma inflicted by these beings who had turned away from their hearts and therefore from Source. What a waste! How could it come to this?

"It is not a waste in itself. You must see it as a whole. And thus, see the chance that is given to each of you to remember who you really are."

"Yes, perhaps, but it's going to be a terrible shock for humans when they learn the truth."

"Not necessarily. It depends on several factors. Do not forget that stellar souls, among others, have gone there to contribute as well. Numerous star nations are involved in this healing/awakening process. And you are one of them."

"Yes, out of love for and in love with Source."

"Exactly."

"So tell me, what happened to your people on Earth, then?"

"When the reptilians—Archons, Annunaki, and Dracos—arrived, we were aware of the plan which had been developed and implemented. At some point, they managed to pervert the minds of many humans and they won back some power. They wanted to exterminate us. We did not want to submit and lose our sovereignty as free and loving individuals, so instead of fighting and clashing with them, and to respect the free choice of all in this plane, we decided to go back to the Pleiades. We are acting in our rightful place and within our abilities, providing care and healing for traumatized souls. We have been accompanying and supporting you all this time on multiple levels. This is how you came to know me, on a rescue mission to Mars. The Dracos had gone too far."

"Wow, that's incredible. I understand so many things better now. It all makes sense. So, everything that humanity is experiencing is actually a direct result of the Orion wars? Living in duality, separation, fear, pride, attachment, judgment, greed, frustration, envy, jealousy, and the need for recognition has but one power and that is to bring us face to face with our own inner demons and to reveal our true selves."

"Absolutely! When you awaken, you remember and that is the beauty of the challenge. For everything is love. Absolutely everything. To awaken means to observe things in depth. Love is always at the root of every choice and every action of every conscious being."

"Hence the importance of remembering who we really are, for we are pure love."

"Precisely! When a species becomes more conscious, it remembers how to express pure love. It remembers how to be love."

"That is beautiful! I'm ever so grateful, Xaman'Ek."

"In Lak'ech Ala K'in, David!"

Temporary Sleep

Xaman'Ek had agreed to put this entire memory sequence of my alternative experience back to sleep, so that I could remember it for myself. This choice may seem incomprehensible to many, but to me, it was a little too early. Even if it is obvious that everything in our experiences is linked, it is better to move forward wisely and without haste. What I was going through in the army at that time was intimately interwoven into this fabric. In addition, Xaman'Ek had managed to thwart some implants. From then on, when I heard certain keywords, I would remember some things related to those words.

It was time to leave Ezahyel and Xaman'Ek. I saw them off warmly. They told me that if I needed anything, they would always be there. Ezahyel also told me that the next few months were going to be difficult in many ways, but that I shouldn't stray far from my center anyway.

I looked them straight in the eyes one last time before they took me down to my bedroom and said: "Mitakuye oyasin, my brothers."

"Mitakuye oyasin," replied Ezahyel.

"In Lak'ech Ala K'in, brother."

I couldn't remember all of what had happened, but I felt so much when they left, and my eyes grew moist. Their broad smiles warmed my heart. The light spiral enfolded me again and it all disappeared.

The Last Months

The weekend had gone by at incredible speed. It was Sunday night and I had stayed for dinner with my parents before heading back to the base. I was able to talk to them about UFOs. Even if I could feel that it was still sticking on several points and that it annoyed them slightly, it didn't matter in the end. The seeds were sown. It was up to them to make them sprout or not.

I started my new job the following morning. The naval firefighters' training was hard but it was a good experience. In the meantime, I had passed my HGV license on the first try. The examiner was impressed by my reverse maneuver while slaloming between the skittles. The weeks went by like a gust of wind sweeping away the dead leaves. Soon, I would not see Olivier again because his service ended at the end of August. During that time, nothing extraordinary happened. Olivier regularly asked me if my article had been published in any of the journals. So far, that was not the case.

Then, it was time for me to go to the holiday camp center on the Gâvres peninsula. I spent the whole month of August there. At first, I was the personal driver of the camp director. I took her into town, to Lorient and to the base for administrative purposes. The problem was that she had phobias about being on the road and she didn't trust me. So, my role as driver came to a halt. They then put me in the kitchen to assist the chef. I didn't mind, as I love discovering new things. But cooking is not an easy job. Preparing breakfast, lunch, and dinner for a hundred children and a dozen adults is not easy. We worked long hours. In the morning, I had to get up at five o'clock. Things got complicated when the chef fell ill. I was on my own for several days. Cooking for lunch and dinner was out of the question. It wasn't my job. And besides, I didn't want to take responsibility in case of food poisoning. Still, they asked me to prepare breakfast every morning. I agreed as I had the rest of the day off. As for the other meals, they had asked a neighboring camp to prepare more food and to have it delivered, while waiting for a new cook. I was delighted with the turn of events. It allowed me to get to know the monitors and the children better. I even participated in some of their activities. But above all, it enabled me to get closer to one particular monitor. I must say that I had been strongly attracted to her since the day I arrived. She had the looks of Gillian Anderson, the actress who plays Dana Scully in The X-Files. She was beautiful. Without realizing it, I fell in love with her.

Anyway, this stay was pure delight and it allowed me to disconnect from the army and from everything else.

Even though I still had to dress in my sailor's outfit, I completely forgot about it.

August also saw the release of Sacred Spirit's "Chants and Dances of the Native Americans" album. This album was a favorite. I vibrated—in every sense of the word—when listening to it. The music features legends and accounts of the Native Americans told in the languages of the Sioux, Navajo, and Pueblo Indians, but also in the language of the Lappish natives (called Sàmi). Their voices are supported by traditional, classical instruments and a fairly distinct use of dance rhythms typical of the time— synthesizers and beatbox. In the US, the album was nominated for a Grammy Award in the Best New Age Album category. In Europe too, the album was a hit in the summer of 1995. It reached the top of the charts in France—and it is quite incredible for this kind of music—thanks to a single named "Yeha-Noha," Wishes of Happiness and Prosperity.

This album reconnected me to that Native American part of me and I listened to it for hours.

Some bonds were formed with certain people. New friendships bloomed, including with some kids, pre-teens who loved to spend time with me whenever they could. There was one boy in particular. He tried to understand things both on human and spiritual levels. I tried to guide him as best I could. He even asked me for my name and address and sent me some mail a little later, telling me how he was doing and checking up on me. It was very touching.

Anyway, the weeks went by at incredible speed again and then, it was time to say good-bye to everyone. Some people were teary-eyed. I was very moved too on seeing them so touched. But something was bothering me. I couldn't see Emmanuelle anywhere. I asked her best friend, Anita, to find out what was going on.

"I really don't know. She left at least an hour ago; she was crying."

I walked in vain almost all around the peninsula to try and find her. I couldn't see her anywhere. What had happened? Was it too painful for her to watch everyone go? Too painful for her to see me leave? I never got an answer. Although she had given me her address and phone number, she never answered my letters and phone calls. Her father always claimed that she was not there. I understood a little later that, precisely out of love, I had to let go and therefore let go of her. Even though I never had an explanation.

The most beautiful proof of love you can give her is to let her go, I was told.

An End to Duties

So, I was back at the base. I had a bit of trouble getting used to it again, to be honest. But my military service ended smoothly. I was even congratulated by the general for my "exemplary" behavior in the camp and I was given an honorary title.

I was able to see Olivier several times. We met at the local restaurants. We gave each other the latest news about UFO sightings. What made me happy was the fact that he hadn't given up. We would continue to see each other even after my service ended. That was really good, as I liked him a lot.

Then, sometime later, it was my turn. The military service was over and I could already feel the release. Olivier was waiting for me at the exit to greet me. He also asked me if I had had any news about my article.

"I do, actually. I had some news from one of the journals' publication managers. He turned the article down. Without giving me any explanation."

"It was to be expected."

"Yes, you're right, Olivier. Some things do bother people. You know what it's like now."

"Yes, I do. I'll never forget what we went through."

"Neither will I."

"See you soon, my friend."

"See you very soon. Take care, my friend."

After the Army

I was finally back home. For good. The army was behind me now—or so I thought. I would keep some great memories of it anyway. Even if the months to come were going to be very trying, both for me and for my parents.

As I was not entitled to unemployment, I had to find a job quickly. As soon as I was registered as a temporary worker, the offers started to come in. So, I found myself working in various sectors of industry. One of my first assignments was in the car industry in the industrial estate of Carquefou. I found myself working in three shifts in a factory making rubber and plastic parts for a French car manufacturer.

One morning, as I was leaving work at 5a.m.—I was on night shift that week—I left the factory and headed for the car park to get my car, as I did every day. I had barely left the industrial estate when, as I halted at a stop sign, I saw a strange red light in the sky that was coming toward me. It seemed to be rather low.

To find out for sure, I got out of my car. The object was above me. Perfectly silent. Triangular in shape and black in color. It continued its descent. It was so close I could almost touch it. A white light intensified from the center of the device. And then, I clearly saw the US AIR FORCE logo. What did it mean? I could watch it for a few more seconds, then it suddenly disappeared.

Anyway, I woke up the next day in my bed at 3:00 a.m., not remembering anything nor how I got home. All I could remember was how closely I had observed this triangular ship, and then my mind just went blank. I would have to do some research to understand what had happened.

I got up, still half-asleep, and headed for the kitchen to have breakfast. My mother greeted me and said that I still looked quite tired.

"Yes, it's been a tough night at work," I replied evasively.

"You got some mail," she said.

"Great! I'll look at it after I've had breakfast and showered."

In the mail was a reply from the second ufology journal I had gotten in touch with. They would publish my article in the next issue. Without realizing it, I let out a cry of joy. I was so excited and thrilled by this news that for a moment, I forgot that there were people around me. The reaction was not long in coming. I heard my mother from the living room: "What's going on?"

"Oh, it's just that I'm going to be published in a journal," I revealed as I joined her.

"In a journal? What journal?"

"It's a journal about UFOs."

"About UFOs?"

I realized that I had told her too much or not enough, so I decided to tell her everything. There was no turning back. Once I had told her everything I had experienced during my military service, including the custody, she was stunned.

It wasn't that she didn't believe me, but I could feel fear surfacing in her.

"You're going to get us into trouble with your nonsense!"

"No, I'm not! Don't worry. Everything's going to be just fine," I said, trying to reassure her.

"Of course, it is! Oh, when your father hears about this!"

"Don't worry. Writing it down and disclosing it will protect me. And besides, I am protected. We are protected."

She had a hard time coming to terms with all this news. I tried to explain it to her as best I could. As she had been opening up to certain things for sometime now, she eventually listened to me and calmed down.

"You'll let me explain this to Dad this weekend, won't you?"

"You want to tell him everything?"

"I do, but not until the weekend. You won't be telling him anything until then?"

"Well ... all right."

"Thanks a lot, Mum."

I trusted her but felt that she was anxious. At the same time, it was understandable. Mothers always worry about their children.

A Death

A few months had gone by and events had continued to occur, one after the other. My parents now knew. I had told them everything, explained everything, including my first encounter with Ezahyel, when we were at the Petit Port in Nantes. I hadn't told them about the fact that I was from elsewhere, though. It was still too early, because my arrival on Earth is somewhat unusual.

Something else happened during that time. One night, while I was sound asleep, I woke up, as I felt a presence in the room. I opened my eyes after a few moments and checked. What a surprise to see that my neighbor, Mr. Joseph, was at the foot of my bed! He was completely surrounded by white light, or he was giving out this light himself. He was smiling broadly. After about a minute, he raised his right hand and gestured as if to wave me good-bye. Then, he disappeared. It took me several minutes to understand the reason for his appearance in my room. He had just passed away.

His soul, before returning to Source, wished to let me know and said good-bye, while making it clear that all was well. And I did feel love surrounding him. The next day, we could expect someone to come and tell us that he had died.

The next morning, I was preparing my breakfast and I kept thinking about what had happened overnight. My mother burst into the kitchen. She looked a little upset.

"I have to tell you something, Mum."

"Yes, I'm listening."

"Last night, something incredible happened. I saw our neighbor, Mr. Joseph, at the foot of my bed. He was made of light. An all-white light. He smiled at me and then waved me good-bye and disappeared."

"It can't be! I ... I saw him too ... he was by the fireplace," she said, dumbfounded.

"Wow, is it true? You saw him too?"

"Yes. I first thought I was dreaming, then ..."

"Wait, Mum, someone's coming to knock on the door."

And within seconds, there was a knock on the door. My mother was all the more surprised. It was Mr. Joseph's son. He told us that his father had died the night before. We offered him our sincere condolences.

My mother still couldn't believe it. We discussed it at length afterward. What a pleasure and a relief it was for me to be able to openly talk with her about it. Despite the circumstances. Now, death is just an illusion.

My Childhood Friend

Since I was back home from the army, I could see my best friend more often. We have known each other since we were kids. In fact, we met through my father. He had a colleague at work who he got on really well with. We used to have regular parties with them on weekends. It wasn't long before my ties with Dave (a pseudo) grew strong, so much so that I immediately considered him a brother.

He had a disability from birth. I never dwelt on that. I saw him fully as a human being. Unfortunately, this was not the case for everyone. You know how cruel people can be sometimes. He suffered throughout his childhood, right up to an advanced age. I always supported and accompanied him. Today, our paths have diverged. After some forty years of friendship and brotherhood, everything came to a halt. There had already been some forerunners. I had warned him twice before that if he continued on the path he was taking, he risked putting an end to our close friendship. The third and final time was unforgiving. I told him that it was all over and that he could not count on me anymore. But I didn't actually think it would be so radical. I was mostly trying to raise his awareness, so that he would awaken, as I had tried the two other times. I have never seen him since. We can't help people, purely and simply because they have to raise their awareness themselves. There is no point in forcing things. Everyone moves at their own pace. May he know, if he reads this book, that he has long been forgiven. My heart and my door are always open.

So, we met each weekend. I went to his house every other weekend and vice versa. Every Saturday, we generally used to go to the city center of Nantes to shop for video games, comics, and figurines, as we were both collectors and drawing enthusiasts. And we ended up at a restaurant and bars in the evening. They were fine moments for sharing.

One fateful Saturday night in August—I'll always remember it, as it was Dave's birthday—we left one bar to go to another that was closing later. I had an urge to pee and told Dave to wait for me, that I was going to relieve my bladder in a tiny, quiet alley.

So, I headed for that fateful alley, which was already quite dark despite the moonlit night. I had hardly finished when I heard a noise. Someone was coming my way. I could hear heavy footsteps. And it sounded a bit metallic at times. I hurried to finish and leave. And then, I hardly had time to turn around when I found myself facing a group of men. There were at least ten of them. And on closer inspection, despite the darkness in the alley, I could see that they were soldiers.

Commandos, even. Hooded and armed with light machine guns. One of them broke away from the group and came closer.

He had stars on his shoulders. He said to me threateningly: "Mr. Rousseau! We know who you are. And you're going to stop playing the wise guy with us."

"What? What are you talking about?"

"You know very well what it's about. Don't play dumb, lad," he retorted casually.

"I have no idea what you mean, man. Who are you? How come you know me?" I had started to talk familiarly to him too.

"You know very well what it's all about. Stop your little game right away."

"No, I don't know! And what gives you the right to threaten me?"

"All right, is that how you take it? You're playing the hotheads, are you? Are you now?" The tension was rising. I heard several soldiers cocking their rifles. They were ready to fire.

"Do you know what will happen to you if you go on with this?"

"I have a slight doubt," I said mockingly.

"Very well! On the count of three, guys!" he said to his battalion as he moved aside.

I stood in front of them. My legs were a bit shaky, I have to say, and I told them: "Go ahead! Kill me! What's stopping you from shooting? Go ahead! Kill me! But know that you will not harm my spirit!"

At the same time, we heard motorbikes starting up in the street. The noise probably disturbed them, because when I turned around, they were gone.

"Phew! Good grief! What the heck is happening to me?" I wondered, with my head down and both hands on my knees, catching my breath.

CHAPTER IX

Surveillance and Threats

After I got a grip on myself, I joined Dave, who was waiting for me.

"Well then? What the heck were you doing? I've been waiting for you for at least ten minutes."

"Yeah … Well, don't even talk about it! I'll explain later. Shall we find a bar? We shouldn't be hanging around here too long. And I need a drink!"

I hardly ever drank alcohol, so when he heard me say that, he knew something wasn't quite right.

"What's wrong? Now you're starting to worry me!"

"Let's find a bar and I'll tell you."

Once we were settled in the back of the room of a new Cuban-style bar, we waited for our order. The music was loud enough for people not to overhear what we were going to talk about. I wasn't very serene. I was looking all around us. My friend was getting more and more nervous. He was stressed, you could tell. At least, I could as I knew him well enough to spot the signs.

Our order came. After the waiter left, I took a big swig of wine and told him everything that had happened. From the army to tonight. He didn't know about my misadventure on the base. Let's just say that he was almost in shock.

"Fuck! All those UFO stories you told me, are they true then?"

"That's what I've been trying to make you understand."

"Fucking hell!"

"Don't worry about it. It's going to be all right."

"All right? You almost got yourself fucking killed! I'm not kidding. I don't want anything to happen to you … I don't want to lose you …"

His words sounded a bit like a death knell. I stayed without saying anything for a long time.

After a second drink, I had cleared my head. Dave had calmed down. But he was still more or less in shock.

"It's like being in a spy movie ..."

"Yeah! Except it's not a movie," I pointed out.

"Maybe you should tell the cops."

"The cops? What do you want me to tell them? Seriously, you think they'll believe me? I'll go to the police station and tell them I'm there to file a complaint. They'll ask me: Yes. Against whom? Er, the French army. And what do you want to file a complaint about? Well, I saw a UFO and they've been threatening me ever since. They'll just have me committed. No, it's out of the question."

"Yeah, put it that way, it's probably not a good idea."

"No, not really. But I understand that you want to protect me and that I protect myself. It's to your credit. But I'll handle it. I have some support, too."

"You could also give up ..."

"Could I? Oh, no, I'm no ostrich or little sheep."

"But what is it that makes you get involved in this?"

"There is nothing making me. I would rather say that it drives me. But that would take too long to explain now."

"Are there still things I don't know?"

"Yes, there are. Careful, it's not against you. There are things I haven't told anyone yet."

"Why not? Not even your parents?"

"Yes, even my parents don't know all of it just yet."

"Why not?"

"Let's just say I prefer to keep it to myself. No one is willing to hear some of these things, at least for the time being, because it goes against everything we have been taught. To take just one example: look at Jesus. He came here to talk about love, brotherhood, and the fact that we are all brothers and sisters ... And you know how he ended up."

"Inconvenient truths?"

"Absolutely! There's no time but the right time, as the saying goes. Jesus is only an example. Many have brought messages and many have disappeared and/or been killed."

"And you think this is deliberate?"

"That's another vast topic. Do you want to get into that kind of discussion now?"

"No, it's true, it's getting late. I didn't see the time pass, what with all this."

"Neither did I."

The bar was closing. It was time to part and go home.

On Sunday morning, I was having breakfast in the late morning when the phone started ringing. My mother answered.

"It's for you. One Olivier," she said.

I was overjoyed and quickly went to pick up the receiver. What a pleasure it was to hear from him. I hadn't heard from him since the army. We were talking about a number of things when I realized that there were strange noises in the phone. At times, I could hear breathing, whispers, and some kind of jingling. It was really strange. Anyway, Olivier and I had agreed to meet again, and he was going to come here on a Saturday.

"Is he your army mate? The one you saw the UFO with?" my mother asked.

"Yes, that's right, it's him."

"You won't be staying here with him. You'll go wherever you want, but not here."

I could feel my mother's fear rising again. And I could understand it. So, I didn't tell her what had happened to me the day before. I didn't want to scare her more.

"OK! No worries. We'll go into town. It will give him the opportunity to discover Nantes," I replied.

"Very good! Oh, by the way, you got some mail yesterday. There's a letter from the army."

"From the army? Where is it?"

"It's there, on the dresser."

"Thank you."

I grasped the envelope and indeed, there was the official logo on it. I opened it, curious to see what they wanted from me. At first sight, it was not a classic letter. All the logos of the army were there: the land army, the air force, and the French navy. I read the content quickly, as the message was short: "Mr. Rousseau, please stop circulating CLASSIFIED DEFENSE information immediately. If not, we will have no choice but take the necessary measures against you."

There was no signature, no stamp or seal of any kind. There

you go, in the eyes of the army and of the state, I was becoming dangerous. I have to say that I was quite affected.

"What's the matter? You look pale," my mother told me.

"Well, how can I put it? The army is threatening me. They want me to shut up."

"Did they threaten you?"

"Yes, look for yourself," I said, handing her the letter. "Oh my God! Oh my! Where are we headed with your stories?"

"And that's not all. I have to tell you something else."

After I told her what had happened to me with the commando group the night before, she was stunned. She angrily nearly ordered me to drop everything. I persisted and told her that I wouldn't. We had a good quarrel that day. I cleared off in my car and only returned in the evening. I hadn't gone far but it was enough for me to take a step back and think. I had reached the Mazerolles plains, on the banks of the Erdre. The place did me good. I reconnected with the elements. And above all, I could talk to Ezahyel, quietly.

The U.P.A.R.O.

"Don't worry, you're protected. Well protected. But I understand that you want to feel safer, from a material and physical point of view. You think of your family in particular."

"I do, Ezahyel. How can I protect myself, my integrity, and the integrity of my relatives?"

"You can do it in many ways."

"Please, give me an example. I don't really know, I'm not detached enough."

"Yes, I can see that. For example, you can set up an organization. Creating a legal entity will protect you in many ways."

"Oh yeah! I hadn't thought of that. That's great. So, I'll have to set up a … uh, ufological organization?"

"Yes, why not. It should allow you to continue doing what you are doing."

"OK! I already have a name coming: UFO Phenomenon Amateur Research Organization. The U.P.A.R.O.! Sounds good, doesn't it? What do you think?"

"It's a good idea."

"I think you need at least two people to create an organization, though. Who am I going to ask to join me in the project?"

"Don't you have an inkling?"

"Yes, I do. I think I do. In any case, thank you for everything, Ezahyel."

"You're welcome."

The U.P.A.R.O. was thus born, at least on paper. All I had to do now was to take the administrative steps. But before that, I had to find the second member and I was not sure that the one I had in mind would accept.

In the meantime, I had understood something else about the strange noises in the phone. I had probably been wiretapped. It confirmed several facts. Olivier had told me the same thing. My parents had repeatedly heard abnormal sounds and lately, I had been having strange dreams every night, about abductions, secret government agencies, and advanced technologies hidden from the public. They were too real and detailed to be merely dreams. The idea of going to a hypnotist became more persistent. I felt I had memories buried in my mind. Only some snatches resurfaced. But what did it mean? Was it all connected?

"Absolutely! Never forget that everything is connected, and that it is all part of a huge web that is woven with invisible yet very real threads, a web of life you are the creator of in each of your experiences."

"Hold on. You mean I created these experiences?"

"Of course you did! Remember the soul's choices. You are all creators and co-creators. Nothing is left to chance."

"I remember very well. Thanks. But why am I seeing the same things every night at the moment?"

"That is because of what you are experiencing in the moment, but also because of your choices."

"Did I choose a life as a secret agent? Did I choose to be kidnapped every night or so? And where do these technologies come from, which I see and use, for some of them, while being unable to put words or labels on them?"

"You did not choose a secret agent's life as you can conceive it in simple human terms. Yet I would say it is equivalent. And yes, you have used 'exotic' technologies. It's up to you to remember that. I remind you that it was at your request that we put certain memories to sleep."

"Is that so? Did I ask for that?"

"Definitely! You did not feel ready to remember all of it."

"Well, it must have been something ..."

"Let's say it covers a long period of your life."

"So, how do I access that memory again?"

"You've given yourself a specific time frame."

"You mean I programmed myself?"

"Yes, you can see it that way. You will soon hear things. You'll hear words, which will be like keys that unlock your memory sequences."

"Can you give me a clue?"

"MK Ultra."

Those words had a strange effect. It told me something, deep inside, but at the same time it seemed negative. I could feel pain resurfacing. There was a painful and unbearable side to it. A very difficult experience to go through. I had no idea how bad it really was, until one day some memories came back to me, and not the least. We shall see this a little further on.

An Unexpected Offer

It was Saturday and Olivier was about to arrive. I had invited my friend Dave to join us so they could get to know each other and he could hear some things from Olivier.

Once everyone was here and introductions were made, we took my car to go to town. We went to a little bar behind Place du Commerce and the FNAC store that Dave and I knew well and where we could have lunch. At the table, the conversation soon turned to the paranormal. Olivier talked about our experiences together, including that fateful police custody. He went on to talk about recent UFO sightings he had made. He also talked about the issue of the noises in the phones. Dave was surprised.

"What? Are you being wiretapped?"

"We have every reason to believe that we are indeed," I replied.

"It's crazy! What do they want from you?"

"Oh, a lot of stuff."

"They're keeping a close eye on us in case we disclose anything that would make them uncomfortable, for example," Olivier confirmed.

While we were still chatting around the table with a coffee, the table suddenly started to vibrate and move by itself. Dave and Olivier were surprised.

"What's going on?" Olivier asked me.

"I think someone is trying to let us know they are there and want to communicate."

The table continued to vibrate and even lifted slightly off the floor at times. We were holding our coffee cups, so that they wouldn't fall and draw attention to us.

"Are you doing that? With your knee?"

"No, I'm not, Dave! No way! Why would I do that?"

When the table started to levitate again, he looked underneath and saw that it wasn't me, and that I was staying still. It scared him a little. I tried to reassure him, but he insisted that we get out of the place, which we did. Once we were out of the bar, Dave and Olivier wished to go to the FNAC store.

"OK, guys. I'm scooting to the tobacconist's to buy a pack of cigarettes and then I'll join you."

"All right! That's fine."

So, I went to the nearest tobacconist's, which was about seven hundred meters away on the corner of Jean-Jacques Rousseau Street. On my way back, I decided to cut through the small alleyway parallel to the one where the bar was located. In this pathway, there often were some homeless people, mostly young ones, so I expected to run into them. Except that I found myself in front of a man wearing a suit—a very classy suit, by the way. He was a short-haired westerner who spoke French with a strong American accent. Strangely enough, the street was empty.

"Mr. Rousseau?"

What was going on now? He knew my name.

"Have no fear, Mr. Rousseau. I'm just here to talk to you."

"Talk to me? Who are you? I don't know you. And how come you know my name?"

"I have an offer for you," he said calmly.

"An offer?"

"Yes! Absolutely! And I'm sure you'll like it."

"Let me be the judge of that."

"Would you like to join a specialized team?"

"Specialized? In what field?"

"Research."

"Research? Research into what? I'm not a scientist nor an archaeologist."

"We know that. Let's say it is research that doesn't fall within the legal and official framework."

"I don't understand … what do you mean?"

"Is it that you do not understand or that you pretend not to understand? Come on, Mr. Rousseau. I expected a little more liveliness and enthusiasm."

"Could you be clear, rather, and not beat around the bush like a fly around a turd?"

"Ah ah … I must admit you're quick at repartee."

"Thank you! What do you want, in the end?"

"Let's say I am opening a door for you to get closer to a subject you are particularly passionate about. Do you understand me?"

I looked around me. There was not a soul, which was strange as there was almost always some traffic around there, especially on a Saturday. How could it be possible? Was this man somehow keeping people away? "Alien presence?"

"Yes, absolutely."

"And what exactly will I be doing in your group or organization?"

"Field investigations of witnesses, recovery of exotic objects if any, as well as photographic and video evidence."

"In short, silencing the witnesses and erasing the traces!"

"That's one viewpoint."

"And what's in it for me if I accept?"

"Privileged access to things that are beyond human understanding."

"Such as?"

"Some of the technologies we develop, for example."

"Like what?"

"I can see what you're trying to do, Mr. Rousseau, and it's shrewd."

"What am I trying to do?"

"You're trying to get information and turn the tide."

"Am I? You're mistaken. I'm just trying to find out what this is all about. I like to know what I'm setting foot."

"I get it. But before I tell you more, I need to know if you'll join us."

"But join you in what?"

"A secret program belonging to another program, which itself belongs to another."

"That's all pretty slim. If you think I'm going to follow you with so little information! How can I be sure you're not something else? Do you have anything to show me?"

He took out a kind of access badge from the inside pocket of his jacket. I could only make out a logo, because he quickly put it back in its place. Oddly, I had a vague feeling that I recognized it.

"Do you belong to a space program?" I asked him.

"Well spotted! You are really perceptive. Let's say that this is just the tip of the iceberg. We work much more in depth. In every sense of the word. That's what the Solar Warden is for."

The Solar Warden. That name sent a shiver down my spine. I had heard it before. But where? I tried not to show that I had recognized the name. For it was a name, I was sure of it.

"That's what it is. So, what do you think? I'm awaiting your decision."

"If I accept your offer, what happens next? In concrete terms?"

"You change your identity. We let people believe you are dead. This will be painful for your loved ones, but it is one of the sine qua non conditions. You won't be able to go back. And then, we'll send you on missions around the world and even beyond."

"Basically, you're asking me to forget my present life, including my close family and friends, so that you can be sure that I will remain silent and keep the secret?"

"In short, yes!"

"Well, no thanks! I'd rather remain who I am than live in lies, silence, and secrecy."

"Are you sure? Do you know what you're missing out here?"

"Yes, I'm sure. This kind of life is not for me."

"Remember, we know who you are."

"Is that a threat?"

The man did not answer me and was already walking away. He was very fast. I tried to catch up with him, but when I reached the street corner, he had disappeared. It was unbelievable. Goodness! Who was that guy?

I suddenly remembered that Olivier and Dave were waiting for me at the FNAC store. I ran to it. When I got to the entrance, I bumped into them. I was surprised and asked them:

"What are you guys doing? Are you going out already?"

"Already? We've been inside for over an hour and we were waiting for you."

"No! Stop it. Are you pulling my leg?"

"No, we're not. Have a look at my watch!"

"Gosh! How can that be?"

"What's going on with you?"

"It's just that I was having a conversation with a guy. I didn't see the time go by."

"A guy you know?" Dave asked.

"No! Not at all!"

"Now you're chatting for over an hour with a guy you don't know?"

"Yeah! I'll explain. But not here."

We went to the botanical garden, not far from there, just to find a quiet corner away from prying ears. Once I had explained to them what had happened to me earlier, they just couldn't believe it. "It's crazy! Aren't they going to leave you alone?"

"As things are, I don't think so, Dave."

"Somehow, it shows we're on the right track. If they're trying to lay their hands on you, it means you're very close to the truth."

"Maybe, Olivier, but which truth? There is more than one."

"About the aliens. He told you so himself, didn't he?"

"He did. But you also know that it's a vast topic. Actually, it makes me think of something else. In order to continue my research, I need to set up an association. Are either of you game for it? Knowing that at least two people are required for this, I thought of you. Setting up an association will protect me and protect us. I called it U.P.A.R.O., which stands for UFO Phenomenon Amateur Research Organization.

"No, I'm sorry, David, but it's not for me," Dave unsurprisingly announced.

"Olivier? What do you think?"

"I don't know. On the one hand, it's very tempting, but on

the other, I hesitate."

"What makes you hesitate?"

"Well … the fact that I still live with my parents, for example."

"Yes, I know. So do I, I remind you. That's the case for everyone here."

"Are you scared of potential retaliation against your family?"

"I have to say I am. Especially with what's been going on for sometime now."

"If you don't want to, I understand. No worries."

"Excuse us, but personally, I think it's getting too dangerous."

"Don't worry about it. I totally get it. No problem and no need to justify yourselves either. I'll find someone else."

"I wish you all the best for the future, David. You're stronger than you look," Olivier said.

"Yeah! You have guts, as they say," Dave concluded humorously.

The day had gone by too quickly. In the evening, it was time for Olivier to go back. He had roughly a two-hour drive. He promised to call me back. Months went by, years went by, and I never heard from him again. Life—our soul—takes us down many paths. In any case, everything is perfect.

"Soon, you will be at the crossroads," Ezahyel said to me without telling me anything else.

The Lone Ranger

Still, I was alone again. How would I set up my association? Who else could I ask to join me? My parents? No. My sister or brother? No, not them either. I was deadlocked. I couldn't see anyone close enough to me to accept such an idea. Should I give it all up? Sometimes I thought about my unknown interlocutor's fateful offer. Part of me would have liked to accept. But there was too much at stake. And above all, I had more and more memories resurfacing and making me think that I had already participated in that kind of program. How could this be? So far, I did not have a clue. It was still too remote. Even if sometimes, some scenes were quite clear and I could see all the details, it was still muddled in my mind.

Sometime later, while researching through books and articles, I came across a topic that captivated me a great deal: the TR-3B.[16] It was a black triangular-shaped aircraft which looked suspiciously like the one I had seen and boarded.

The last time, I had seen it so close that I could make out the US AIR FORCE logo on it. Then, I had a blackout.

"It's an aircraft of terrestrial origin," Ezahyel told me.

"What? How so?"

"They designed it by using reverse engineering."

"Using technology from elsewhere?"

"Exactly."

"The Roswell crash?"

"Among others. There have been many others."

"Hey, but that reminds me of the wave of UFOs in Belgium and France in 1990. All those who could observe it described a black triangular-shaped craft. Was it? Was it a TR-3B?"

"Yes, it was. There was not just one, by the way."

"Wow, what were they trying to do?"

"A show of force."

"Unbelievable! By letting everyone think it came from somewhere else?"

"Absolutely. Somehow, that was the point of their maneuver."

"The Greys have ships that look like this. I've seen some."

"Yes, that's true."

"Were they trying to pass themselves off as them?"

"In the eyes of some in your ufology community, they were indeed."

"And by doing so, they wanted to bring discredit and doubt and misinformation ..."

"Again, that is correct."

"Thank you for everything, Ezahyel. Genuinely."

"You are welcome."

---

16   The Northrop TR-3 Black Manta is reputed to be a US Air Force secret spy plane which was designed in the 1980s. It is said to be part of the "Black Programs," but its existence is officially denied to this day.

New Disclosures

That night, sleep came quickly. I went to bed with the images of the TR-3B in my mind, thinking about what Ezahyel had told me. Soon after, I was in the arms of Morpheus.[17]

Then, in the middle of the night, I suddenly woke up, thinking I had a dream. But the most incredible thing about all this was that I kept seeing amazing things. How was this possible? A dream in full consciousness? A projection of my mind? Of my higher consciousness?

In any case, it was all too real. I felt as if I were in a movie of some sort, except that the movie in question was live and I was the lead actor. My immersion in this earlier event in my life lasted at least a good hour. Everything I saw confirmed not only what I thought and felt, but it also enabled me to remember many things about myself, my childhood, the missing times—which were numerous, the abductions by the Greys, the very advanced technologies I had already used, my encounters with many nations from the four corners of the galaxy, as well as top-secret programs, which even many politicians do not know exist and which cost billions. In order not to forget anything, I decided to write everything down, while it was still fresh in my mind.

Secret Space Programs

Here are the events as I experienced them, and as they came back to me:

When I was eight years old, a dark triangular spacecraft—a TR-3B—flew over me. Some kind of beam of light came down from it and sucked me in. It was as if I were suddenly floating up to the mysterious craft and when I got inside, I found myself with some American soldiers. One of them spoke French. I was told that everything was fine, that I had nothing to worry about. I didn't feel any movements, but the ship was flying very fast. Within minutes, we were above a desert in America and

---

17   In Greek mythology, Morpheus, the god of dreams, is the son of Hypnos, the god of sleep, and of Nyx, or Nox in Latin, the goddess of the night.

the next moment, we were in a huge underground facility. And there were many people inside: doctors, scientists, soldiers, who were armed as if there were a war brewing. I was told again that everything was fine. That I had nothing to fear. Oddly enough, I felt no fear. Various feelings were intertwined. I was surprised without really being surprised. I had the feeling that I had been there before and that I already knew this place. I had a clear sense of déjà vu.

The senior officer who had been with me since the moment I came aboard the ship told me that I was now to be taken for some medical examinations and tests. He told me again that everything would be fine.

We had taken a lift and we were going down. I don't remember how many levels there were, but it took us long minutes to go down, so much so that I wondered if it would ever stop.

The doors opened and we found ourselves in a sort of corridor. On each side were armed soldiers. When we went out, we turned left. There were no openings, no natural light, only artificial lights strewn along the walls of the corridor on either side. Then, we came to a door and my "guide" took a badge out of his pocket, saying: "This is a special badge, issued only to a very few people."

The door opened. The room looked a bit like an operating theater in a hospital. There were a couple of doctors/scientists and another two soldiers. I looked around me, there were screens I had never seen before, with a whole bunch of devices I could not recognize. The senior officer asked me to go and sit down on a chair facing two screens. The screens looked almost transparent when viewed up close. I was told that I would be connected to a computer via hi-tech sensors for analysis and measurement.

"There'll be no pain," I was told. "Just routine checks."

Two sensors were put on my temples and another in the middle of my forehead. They had no wires and emitted intermittent blue lights. I saw my head and then my brain appeared on the screens. One of the scientists cracked a smile as he looked at one of his colleagues.

"That's it, we're ready!" he said to everyone. My military guide then said to me: "Very good, David! Now relax, breathe calmly. We will analyze your brain and its activity. Everything will be fine! Right, close your eyes for a moment and take a deep breath!"

After a few seconds, I heard a woman's voice: "David, can you hear me?"

I opened my eyes and looked around. I couldn't see a woman in the room.

"Can you hear me, David?" she asked me again.

Seeing that she wasn't here, I decided to answer telepathically.

"Yes, I can hear you. But I can't see you."

"Don't worry, everything is fine. I am not with you, but we can communicate."

"Are you in a room next door?" I asked her.

"No, I'm not! In fact, I'm far away from you, and very close at the same time."

"What do you mean? Are you dead?" I was beginning to think that I was talking to a spirit.

"No, no, I'm not. I'm not dead, I'm very much alive," she said, laughing.

Around me, I could hear the scientists bustling about and one of them said, "This is pretty incredible! Look at this activity! We have only rarely seen this."

My military guide was smiling broadly.

"Keep going!" he ordered them.

In fact, not only could they see everything that was happening on the screens, but they could also hear my conversation with this mysterious woman. Probably through those earpieces they were wearing, which must be connected to the sensors.

"But where are you?" I asked.

"David, I am more than one hundred and eighty-six thousand miles away from where you are, and yet I can hear you as if I were standing next to you."

And then, I didn't really know why, but it became clear to me and I said to her: "You are not on Earth!"

There was a relief in her voice: "Indeed. I'm not on Earth with you. I am on the Moon!"

"On the Moon!?"

"Yes! Don't worry. The general will explain everything. And welcome among us. We'll meet again, very soon. Good-bye, David!"

The communication was over and I could see that everyone around me was smiling. They were talking a lot. The exchanges were intense.

The general took the sensors off me and said: "Come! Get to your feet and follow me! We need people like you, David, people who have the ability to communicate with their minds or thoughts. If you agree, you will be part of something unique and have an out-of-the-ordinary experience. Come with me, I'll show you what it's all about and introduce you to some 'special people.'"

We headed back to the lift. The two armed soldiers in the corridor started to walk and followed us.

As he perceived my concern, the general said to me: "Don't worry about it. It's just a security measure. They are armed like this to prepare for any eventuality and/or threat. You will understand this better by yourself shortly. Don't be scared, though, as you will meet 'people' that you have never seen before. Some of them are very impressive. But don't be intimidated, because they can pry into your mind.

"Even though you are only eight years old, I know you understand me. From now on, your life will change, David! Are you ready?"

I nodded. We took the lift again and went down a few more levels.

"Just so you know, you can refuse to continue at any time and go home. We are not forcing you to do anything. Even if the way we brought you here is a bit brutal and sudden, you always have a choice. So, I'll ask you again: are you ready?"

"Yes, I am," I assured.

But at the same time, a flood of thoughts, feelings, and emotions had engulfed me. I was thinking more particularly about my parents, my family, and my friends. It was as if I sensed that I would not see them again for a long time. And on the other hand, it was as if I felt like I belonged here. Something resonated within me.

The general snapped me out of my thoughts. We had gone out of the lift and into a corridor similar to the previous one. And there, in front of a sturdy metal door, he told me: "We have arrived, David! From the moment you walk through that door, there is no turning back. So, it's up to you now to decide if you really want to go on."

"I do!" I answered him without a second thought.

"Very well! Perfect, David! So, get ready to enter a new world, unknown to almost everyone. Life as you know it no longer exists or at least, forget everything you have known so far because, in actual fact, it is all different. But you already know that, don't you?"

"You mean the ETs I saw not long ago?"

"Haha ... that's what you call them ... Yes, that's it. And you'll see for yourself that there are many of them, in various forms and appearances. So, are you ready?"

"Yes!"

This time, the badge alone was not enough to open the door, he had to enter a long code onto the box. With a dull metallic creak, the thick door opened. At first, I could not make out anything, as the light was so bright.

The general said to me: "Let's wait a couple of minutes while they finish their tests. The light will go back to normal."

I could hear people on the other side. Lots of movement too. And above all, a sound. A kind of vibration that resonated and almost blocked my ears. The intense light had finally faded to nothing.

"Just a few more seconds and we can go," the general said.

We went through the door and into a huge room. It was really crowded. And in the center in particular, there was a group of beings who were not from here. Some looked like the ones I had seen sometime before. Others were almost human. They were all surrounding a strange object that emitted pulses of light.

All of a sudden, I realized that they were all looking at us.

"Don't be afraid! We'll introduce ourselves later. I'm taking you to see someone in particular."

We walked across the room to a door and into another room.

There was a woman with long blond hair, two small grey-skinned people, and another soldier, a colonel. They seemed to be talking. But I could already sense a disagreement. The tension was palpable. And above all, the hairs on the back of my neck stood up, as if to warn me that something was wrong or that there was a danger.

The general spoke: "This is the little boy I was telling you about. His name is David."

"Hello, David. Welcome!"

This woman with shiny blond hair had just spoken to me in

my mind. Her voice was soft and warm. But there was something different about her.

"You are not human?"

"Not in the sense that you mean, indeed not. I come from far away, beyond the stars."

The grey beings did not seem happy with my presence, they looked at me and probed me with their huge black eyes. They were trying to get into my mind or my thoughts. The general was right. Yet without knowing how, I managed to keep them out of my mind. What really worried me was my feelings. I still had goosebumps. The "Nordic" woman, apparently that's what they called themselves, reassured me with loving thoughts.

The colonel and the two Greys—again, it was the Nordic woman who told me they were called that, and that they came from Zeta de Reticuli—seemed to be having virulent exchanges. There was something they disagreed about. The colonel took a device out of his pocket. It looked like a miniature screen. When he touched it with his fingers, images and graphics appeared. He showed it to the Zetas as he continued talking.

Then, I noticed that there was some noise to the right, at the back of the room. It was dark there. I could see two soldiers with guns in their hands. But behind them was someone else. A very tall and strong being. I could see his silhouette. My hair stood on end again. Now I understood where it was coming from. This huge being was full of hate, anger, and violence. I could feel it. He came out of the shadows. The soldiers tried to make him step back. He was still moving forward. He had incredible strength.

And then, I got a little scared. He was at least ten feet tall. And he looked like a big lizard. His skin was brown, scaly, and shiny. He stared at me. He was really angry. The soldiers ordered him to back off, but he wouldn't. He kept moving forward. The general ordered them to shoot if he took another step. In vain. He kept moving forward, pushing the two soldiers aside with a gesture. They were about to fire, but their rifles were snatched from their hands. The general stood in front of me. As if to protect me. He was about to fire when suddenly a strange sound was heard.

A blue sphere appeared out of nowhere. Strangely, the reptilian had started to back off. He seemed as surprised as we were. The sphere came and stood between us and him. I could catch sight of someone inside. He seemed to be blue as well. There was a great light emanating from this being, a great loving force. He was so radiant, it was unbelievable. It was a being from the spheres, a Blue Avian. This is what I would learn a little later. The exchanges with these beings, as with many others by the way, are just incredible.

The being emerged from the sphere, which suddenly disappeared. He moved toward us, not caring about the reptilian, who kept away. The general nodded and put his left hand over his heart. I did the same. The being was smiling. He had such a presence. It would be impossible to describe him in words. He was at least eight feet tall; he was humanoid in shape but with notable differences. He had big round eyes, where several colors merged. His hair almost looked like feathers. In fact, it had feathers all over his body, at least what I saw of it. He had almost no nostrils, only two holes above his mouth, which was similar in shape to a bird's beak. He was beautiful. Very beautiful. In every sense of the word.

"Welcome to you, Kie'Teir! My name is Kon'Ti'Ra," he said directly into my heart.

"Thank you very much! I am delighted to meet you," I replied.

It didn't strike me straight away, but had he just called me Kie'Teir? I was overcome with emotion. Tears began to run down my cheeks. Yes, Kie'Teir was my name. How did he know it?

"We will meet again very soon," he told me.

Then, he looked at the general again and greeted him. Next, the blue sphere reappeared and a second one arrived.

The reptilian, who was no longer moving, was drawn inside. They both disappeared in a flash.

"Wow …" I let out. I was at a loss for words.

"Yes! That's something, isn't it? These Blue Avians always have the same effect, every single time," the general said.

CHAPTER X

An Unsuspected Reality

Since this flashback, many memories resurfaced in my mind. I saw myself traveling from mission to mission for this very special unit. Sometimes, I was accompanied by military personnel, sometimes by beings from elsewhere, such as Blue Avians, Pleiadians, Arcturians, Lyrians, etc., but also by my brother from the Pleiades, Xaman'Ek of the ancient Mayans. He was involved in rescue and healing operations. That's how I got to know him, within these secret space programs. Although the Mayans are not part of it, they collaborate, if I may say so, in a sort of galactic/terrestrial alliance.

The reptilians, who are at the origin of the artificial matrix on Earth, are the cause of many misdeeds. The Dracos in particular. They made a deal with the Germans before the Second World War. In exchange for knowledge and technology, they received human beings—men, women, and children—whom they bartered away or violently assaulted before feeding upon them, or else they kept them as slaves. For the thousands of years they have been around, they have maintained the illusion of separation and duality thanks to their technology and the artificial matrix I mentioned before, in order to maintain power and control over human beings. They—and the other involutionary entities—are at the root of false beliefs, religions, and dogmas used to enslave mankind and rule them in fear.

Of course, undoing all those ancient patterns of mental, emotional, and spiritual manipulation will not be easy for many. But we must remember that all this is an illusion, for there is no separation. They have led us all along to believe the opposite to keep us away from our center, that is to say from our hearts. On the soul level, the reptilians have cut themselves off from their hearts and have come to forget themselves completely. So, they have cut themselves off from Source, pure and simple. Today, many of them still refuse to evolve into the fifth dimension and into love.

The Orion wars they started had the same motive. Their system was rising in vibration and an involutionary entity influenced them to reverse the trend. As a result, it succeeded in lowering the frequencies to block them in the fourth and third dimensions. What we are experiencing on Earth is a direct result of the Orion wars. They knew that our world would also evolve, but they refused to accept this new cycle coming from the great central sun and they did everything possible to keep us in the third dimension, thus slowing down the spiritual uplift of humanity.

As a result, the Earth was quarantined by the great intergalactic council. The reptilians had gone too far and were no longer allowed to leave the Earth. No other involutionary entities were allowed in either. Alliances were formed between humans and highly evolved beings to carry out the liberation of Gaia and of its inhabitants. It had been going on for too long. Today, we are at the crossroads. Here is a text I shared on my Facebook page in April 2020:

As you know, we are currently in the midst of a dimensional transition. We are already in the fourth dimension. The current increase in energies automatically updates the vibrations in your chakras or energy centres. The current energies serve in revealing old emotions of upset that you may have.

Observe them, but without soaking them up. Accept them and allow them to detach from you and rise in love. Remember that the key is to stay centred in your heart. To reach the fifth dimension, you must be fully who you really are in the present moment.

Vibrationally and energetically speaking, the Earth has already moved into the fifth dimension. And many souls have already joined her. Many people know this and already live in this dimension of love in their hearts.

Remember that everything is frequency and vibration. The fifth dimension is a higher state of being in which you live from the heart and in the heart, in the vibration and frequency of love.

As you now know, we are at a crossroads. Hence the importance of making your choice, truly.

The choice to continue living in the three dimensional world and duality, or the choice to remain centred in the heart, to welcome love and to raise your vibration to a higher state of being.

Many people ask me how to reach the fifth dimension. I would answer this: The answer is within you. It really is. There is nothing to do, there is only to be.

All souls have been through this evolutionary process—before and elsewhere, and know it well. Many forgot this when they went down into the third dimension. The illusion of separation, duality, the ego and rational mind have kept you in this state of being through the artificial matrix. Many are also awakening at this time, during this transition.

Do you understand why this period of lock down related to COVID-19 is essential?

It allows a great many of you to review their priorities and to recentre. It results in more awareness for you. So, you remember who you really are more and more every day.

There are those who fully remember who they are and why they are here. They are guiding or accompanying you through this dimensional transition. These people are all mostly Walk-Ins, Stellar Souls, Starseeds, Indigos, Lightworkers or Light Warriors.

They sowed seeds of love and light on your path. Today, all these seeds have germinated and/or are germinating, and are coming to life in the hearts of many, so that the beautiful flower of love can expand, radiate and diffuse like a sun.

For, be that as it may, this is what we are. Pure love. This is what our soul is. It cannot be otherwise.

So, you don't have to do anything. You just have to be.

In order to be able to live in the fifth dimension, you first have to live it within you, in your heart.

This is how the shift will happen. And only this way.

New Threats

A few months later, I had managed to set up my association, thanks to a guy I knew in my town, who was to become one of my best friends. I must say that he was a bit of a hothead. He was fearless. He wasn't really interested in the UFO topic, but he believed in them. So, he agreed to become my official treasurer, even though I was in charge of everything. I didn't want to bother him with the paperwork. After all, he was doing me a big favor.

The U.P.A.R.O. was coming to life. At long last.

In just a few weeks of existence—I must say I had advertised in two magazines—I began to receive a lot of mail. Most of it was testimonies. All these people from my region had seen unknown objects in the sky. And they had many questions. I was so happy to receive all these letters, they warmed my heart. There were two cases that actually stood out, if I may say so. They were so interesting that I managed to get interviews with both witnesses. One of them, a woman, remembered being abducted. We had agreed to meet so I could interview her. She had suggested a small bar in the center of Nantes.

"It will be very quiet there, you'll see," she had told me on the phone.

She did not wish to do this at home because of her children, which I understood very well. On D-day, I met an ordinary-looking woman. She was down-to-earth, spontaneous, and she made no fuss. I just trusted her. We sat in the back of the bar and it was true that it was quite nice, with very little noise and some lounge music in the background, so no one could disrupt our conversation. I asked her a few questions and joked around to put her at ease and lighten the mood.

She then told me her story. I listened carefully and took notes as she went along. It was troubling how she remembered some of the details, especially the egg retrieval. But what struck me most in her story was when they—the Greys—brought children to her, three of them.

"These are your children," they told her.

"Wow, that's unbelievable! How did you feel then? What did you feel?"

"I couldn't explain it, but I did feel this connection to them. A mother-child bond. I was convinced that they were really my children. I felt it in my gut, in my heart. It was pounding in my chest. They are different from us. So very different. They told me that thanks to my eggs and all the extractions, they had managed to create hybrid beings, between us and them."

"You say there were three children? Girls? Boys? I don't know if you can put it that way …"

"There was a girl and two boys. But they use the terms 'females' and 'males.'"

"Do they? Very interesting. And did they say anything to you?"

"Yes! Yes! In my head … I heard my daughter's voice … I heard her voice in my head … Her big dark eyes were staring at me and I felt tenderness. And then, she said to me, 'Mother, we are so happy that we can see you at last.' And she took me in her arms. My God! I was holding her in my arms and the emotion rose, so strong and indescribable in human words and even in feelings, and I burst into tears."

Tears were running down her cheeks. The emotion was great and still very much alive in her.

"Excuse me," she said.

"Please, Sophie.[18] There's nothing to be embarrassed about. It's perfectly normal. Let your emotions flow. Don't hold them back."

"Thanks."

"I thank you. Honestly, it's a pleasure to talk to you."

"The crazy thing is that I feel I can tell you everything. I'm not used to opening up like this, especially with a stranger. Don't get me wrong."

"No, no, no worries. I understand you. Believe me, I do. I've been abducted many, many times too, you see. So, I understand all these feelings, all these emotions intertwined in you. But we're not here for me, let's go on, if you don't mind."

Our conversation lasted three to four hours. It's amazing how time can fade away when you're caught up in something that you find utterly interesting, and her testimony was so fascinating.

18   Sophie is a pseudonym.

When we parted, I thanked her warmly and invited her to call me back if she wished to do so. She gladly accepted.

Then, I headed to the Baco Embankment car park where I had left my car. I took the time to walk through the streets of Nantes. I liked this city, I don't know why. Good energy? Good vibes? I guess so. Yet, I couldn't stand the noise of the traffic and the hustle and bustle of modern man. Paradoxical. But anyway, something strange happened again. I had lost track of time while wandering the streets for an hour.

One hour had vanished! But how could it be? I tried to remember what I had done during that time. But I just could not remember. I realized I was in Graslin square. I was almost back to where I started. I couldn't believe it. I took the Jean-Jacques Rousseau Street to go back in the right direction. And then, when I got to the small alleyway in which I was threatened, I had an irresistible urge to go for a pee. I had no choice but to go. Except that this time, I had no time. I faced another group of commandos, who split up to surround me. And the verdict was spoken: "Mr. Rousseau! You are a dead man!"

"What? What the hell do you want from me?"

"We know your every move. If you keep talking about anything at all, you're a dead man! Is that clear?"

"I really don't know what you're talking about. You know what? I don't actually give a damn."

"Yes, get smart with us and your parents will have to write an obituary soon."

"Your threats don't scare me. Because unlike you, I know that death is just an illusion. Our spirit is eternal and you will never harm mine. So, go ahead, get it over with!"

I closed my eyes and opened my arms, offering them my life.

I could not hear anything, no sound, nor the breath of my assailants. I opened one eye and then the other. They had gone.

Life Is Movement

The years went by and the least I can say is that events kept occurring. The more experiences I gained, the greater my awareness. I remembered who I really was a little more each time. It enabled me to remain constantly in my center, in my heart. It resulted in anchoring my loving energy to the Earth.

Ezahyel had often spoken to me about the importance of refocusing, of fully aligning, heart, mind, and soul, of loving ourselves unconditionally in order to love others in the same way, and of not letting ourselves be filled by external things. In this way, we are able to accept more easily what we are going through. We show more detachment, resilience, patience, and true humanity. We understand even better that we are part of this Great Whole we are all in. And that in this Great Whole, there is no separation, no judgment, no dual aspect whatsoever, for all is love.

Once you become aware and awaken who you really are, the first thing that strikes you is that life is light, so much lighter. You also notice that everything is movement and that if you resist these movements, your experience will become harder and heavier, as the mind immediately clings to what it knows and thinks is reality, when it is only an illusion. What you resist persists. Conversely, the more you are in the heart, the more creative your thoughts and the more the miracle will take place, for you will create your life instead of being subjected to it. You will regain your power. You will regain your sovereignty. Your freedom to be who you really are and your freedom to love fully and unconditionally. For such is love: Free, Unconditional, Universal, Multidimensional and, above all, Creative.

White Buffalo Woman

One summer evening, while I was lying on the grass in my parents' garden and watching the stars, I heard a thunderstorm in the distance. I didn't mind, because I loved watching and listening to them. As the minutes passed, the rumblings got closer. The sky began to light up everywhere. It was splendid. There was a great flash of light above me while I was still lying on the ground. Then, I saw a shape come out from the imposing cloud there. I paid close attention to it and did not let it out of my sight even for a moment. It was energetic and above all, it was alive. I don't know how I knew this, yet I could feel it. And suddenly, the form took on the appearance of a huge eagle. His eyes were blue and bright, as if electric. Two bolts of lightning shot out of them. "Wow!" I gasped. I got to my feet. The eagle was still there, powerful and majestic. He turned his head toward me. His gaze pierced me, in every sense of the word. He saw me as I really was, without a doubt. He did not speak directly to me but sent me sensations, emotions, rather. I could feel an intense and luminous love radiating from him. It was unbelievable. Somehow, something connected me to him. I could feel it deep inside me. My cells had started to vibrate in a way I didn't know. As if they were electrified.

"Who are you?" I asked him.

I had no answer. While gazing at him, I asked him again: "What is your name?"

And then, after a low rumble, he said to me in a powerful voice that echoed throughout the surrounding area: "Wakinyan!"[19]

His name had got into my being, right to my heart. I felt a sensation that was now quite familiar. A spiral of energy enveloped me and my spirit began to fly through space-time. I found myself in a not-so-distant past. There was a village of at least a hundred teepees. It was a beautiful sight to behold. These nomadic dwellings were in perfect affinity with the environment. There was a great joie de vivre, a peacefulness filled with respect and beauty. In short, it was harmony. The Mnicoujou people were about to celebrate something. It was the end of the summer. Here and there, you could see the first leaves changing color on the trees, heralding autumn. But it was still warm. The sky was threatening in the east. Cornbread and buffalo meat were cooking on the fires. The scents wafted to my nostrils. There was also some sage burning for fumigation. I felt such a sense of well-being.

A little later, when everyone had eaten, sharing and listening, the shaman said to the gathering: "Hau oyate![20] Today is a beautiful day to live. And we are going to thank the spirits and our Mother Earth for this. Hecetu welo![21] Mitakuye oyasin."

19   It is pronounced "waki-han." It means "thunderbird" in Lakota Sioux.

20   It means "Greetings, dear people" in Lakota Sioux.

21   Hecetu welo is pronounced "echetu welo." It means "I have spoken."

Shouts of joy and approval were heard throughout the village. Drums began to be heard. The beats matched the heartbeat. The ground and our bodies vibrated with them. It was powerful. Then, an equally powerful chant rose above the drums and the plain. It was so beautiful that I didn't realize that tears were streaming down my cheeks.

I guess the drumming had covered everything else, because I became suddenly aware that the storm was right above us and was getting louder and louder. The lightning flashes intermittently illuminated the drummers, singers, and dancers, making the scene mysteriously more beautiful and intense. The drums dropped in rhythm to one single beat every four seconds. A new chant began. I had goosebumps. I recognized that thank-you song; it was Wakinyan Oyate. The song of the Thunderbird. I sang vigorously, accompanying the people in this magnificent loving energy. And then, Wakinyan showed himself. Lightning flashed from his intense blue eyes. All kinds of shouts began to be heard across the plain. I was shouting too, letting out all my emotions. Tears streamed down my face. There was so much beauty there. Beauty that humans could generally not understand. Unless they had walked the Red Road.[22]

For a second, my eyes were drawn to a strange glow a few hundred yards away from us. Strangely enough, no one but me seemed to have noticed it. The glow faded away and was replaced by a beautiful white buffalo. What an incredible sight! And for a short while, I thought it was indeed a vision—a major thing in Native American cultures—and that, as it was my vision, I was the only one who could see it. The glow reappeared again for a few seconds and then disappeared. I couldn't believe it. There was a woman, dressed in a long white deerskin dress and a kind of buffalo blanket or cloak, also white in color, which she wore over her shoulders. Two eagle feathers hanging from her long, raven-black hair fluttered in the wind. She was holding an object in both her hands. I realized that I was now very close to her. Had she moved without me noticing? Or was I so fascinated and intrigued I didn't pay attention?

---

22   The Red Road is a spiritual road and defines a certain way of living one's life. In accordance with all that surrounds us, we connect to our heart and to the heart of the Great Whole and of the universe. Everything is one. Mitakuye oyasin.

In any case, I was close enough, about a meter away, to feel the bliss of what she was radiating. Her beauty was like no other. There was such a power of love emanating from her, incredible both in its intensity and gentleness. She had a broad, powerfully loving smile. Her eyes were deep and full of light. I was mesmerized.

"My dear son, I am so happy to have you back. My heart is filled with joy and happiness. What a wonderful moment, that I honor with this gift."

She handed me the object gently. It was a white deerskin case, half of which was embroidered with rainbow-colored beads depicting a star. The smell of the tanned hide that made up the bag wafted up to my nostrils. What an incredible scent. I already knew these scents and it felt so good to smell them again. She burned a small clutch of sage and directed the smoke toward me, then circled me four times in prayer and thanksgiving. Even the vibration of her voice moved me to tears. Everything about her touched me. I couldn't understand why, until I remembered. With my heart pounding in my chest and my voice trembling, but without hesitation, I whispered: "Mother? Mother, is that you?"

And she took me in her arms. Now I was sobbing.

"Yes, it's me. It is me, my beloved son."

"Oh, Mother, I've missed you so much! Where have you been?"

"I have always been here with you. But you didn't see me until now. You had forgotten me."

"How could I forget you?"

"Coming down to Earth and to its third-dimensional density made you forget a lot of things. And you had to have certain experiences that would bring you back on the path. By taking the Red Road, you took that path, the path of remembrance. And that is why I am here now. You have connected with the part of you that is fully what it really is. Now, son, you will remember many things that you have experienced beyond this world, you will remember why you chose to come down to this beautiful planet. You will understand that all your earlier experiences within the Pleiades during the great Orion wars prepared you to come here to fulfill your purpose in this magnificent Earth Plan. The bag I have given you contains a cannunpa wakan.[23] I have hand-carved and

23   It translates to sacred peace pipe and is pronounced "chanoumpa

sculpted it for you from the sacred red stone. Its pipe represents the divine feminine and its bowl the divine masculine. When it is put together, it means the unity and oneness of hearts, the energies merging together, recreating the symbiosis and harmony of the Great Whole. Smoking the peace pipe connects you to the Great Spirit, to the Creative Source and thanks to the breath, inhale and exhale, you join the breath of life through the smoke, thus raising your prayers, your creative thoughts."

"Mother, I now remember the sacred power of the cannunpa. You could not have given me a greater gift. I am honored and humbled. You have all my gratitude and appreciation. And my eternal love, dear Mother."

"My son, you are loved beyond words, beyond the four winds and the four directions. Both on Earth and beyond."

"Oh, Mother, I have missed you so much! I love you."

"I love you, son. I love you, Wanbli Ska."[24]

She had taken me in her arms again. She exuded and radiated so much love that I wanted this moment never to end.

"Thank you from the bottom of my heart. Thank you for everything," I whispered in her ear.

"Stand in your light," she said to me with love and tenderness.

Then, she disappeared into a kind of light vortex and I stood there in a state of complete bliss for a long time. Tears ran down my cheeks again.

What an incredible evening! I was not going to forget it any time soon. It would always be etched in my memory and in my heart. What a wonderful experience it is to be reunited with your "original" mother and to feel that she is quite close again. I have to say that I was pretty proud. White Buffalo Woman was my mother. I felt so many things that it was impossible to put them into words. It was a whole, utter elation of my senses.

Once I was back into my avatar, I smoked one last cigarette in my parents' garden before going to bed. I felt so light and carried away that I almost felt as if I were gliding. I gazed up at the sky, letting the wisps of smoke rise, filled with my loving thoughts. Tears flowed out from my eyes again. There was only one thing I could do: give thanks.

I stood up with my arms open, palms facing the universe, waran."

24   Wanbli Ska is my spiritual name and it means "white eagle."

and I sang in Lakota, not knowing the language, a chant full of strength and love, straight from the heart.

Stellar Souls

As we near the end of this book—already!—I think it is fundamental to come back to some points, for everything is but a circle. In this first book of Beyond Our World, my first wish was to share my experiences, my life story with you. At least part of it. For you will understand that I cannot relate everything in one go—it would be a doorstop. So, it is my personal choice to proceed in this way and to separate my story into several volumes. Some of my experiences are more vast and complex, more dense and intense, and I have only touched upon them here, at least for some of them. I will detail and explain them more thoroughly in the next books. What's more, as nothing is set and all is movement, I let my soul guide me and inspire me according to my memories in the present moment. As I mentioned in the first pages, I have no precise plan concerning the creation of this manuscript, I only go with the flow of my feelings, intuitions, and heart especially.

So, in short, I have been conscious of not belonging to this world since my early childhood and I will tell you why. I have no memory of the life I lived through this body from my birth until the age of six, because it was not me. Another soul animated this avatar with its breath of life. We had agreed to this experience by mutual consent. This other soul had chosen to do it out of unconditional love. It was to animate this human body with life before I arrived, in order to enable me to remember who I am and not forget everything, as is often the case when we descend to Earth and to the third dimension. There was what some people call an incoming-soul and outgoing-soul process. A sort of transmigration of souls, if you like. So, I am what is called a Walk-In. I am a stellar soul from the Great Central Sun, which has come to Earth during this dimensional transition to support the ascension process. Other Starseeds are also Walk-Ins. Maybe you know some of them personally? Yet, you may not be aware that there is such a person in your family or friends. If such a person did not tell you that he or she was a more evolved entity, you could not figure it out through observation.

Stellar souls, in any case, use this process of inhabiting a body without going through the birth and re-learning stage, so that they can remember who they are as soon as possible and can become aware of their "life missions" again. I do remember this transfer of souls and my arrival very well. I would like to take this opportunity to thank the outgoing soul once again. I have seen it several times. It chose to go through birth again to start a new life experience. I will not mention its name here, but it will definitely recognize itself.

At the beginning of this book, in the introduction, I recounted my memories as Kie'Teir when, out of love, I made the choice to come and assist Earth in her evolution/ascension process. What you should know is that at this dimensional level—from the ninth dimension on—bodies are pure light and energy. However, we can keep the appearance we had before, as is the case for me and my family among the nation of the Elders. We can shape our bodies as we wish, so to speak, just as we can lower them in frequency to experience a denser body. That is what happened to me. It is a whole process, by the way. Before descending into much denser worlds, we have to lower our vibration. Starting from the Great Central Sun, I moved toward the Pleiades for a smooth transition. I therefore incarnated with a less luminous body to prepare for my coming to Earth. My Pleiadian family was already waiting for me; they had accepted my arrival among them with great love, and the woman who was to carry the embryo that would become my avatar was Pte San Wi, White Buffalo Woman.

She already knew the little blue planet well, as she had come there several times to meet the North American Native Americans, and in particular the Lakotas, as they descend from the Pleiadians. She had offered them the cannunpa wakana, or sacred pipe, as well as spiritual advice.

But if this is my first time on Earth, how can I explain my previous incarnation as a Lakota Mnicoujou? Well, I was not actually really there. It was more of a projection of my consciousness. Now you know that the Native Americans have a close connection with the Pleiadians, as they are their earthly descendants. So, from the Pleiades, by mutual agreement with the soul that animated that body, my consciousness lived its experience with it and through it remotely.

So, I had all the physical, emotional, spiritual, etc., sensations as if I were really there. You will surely remember this passage where I talk about Wounded Knee. You also know how that ended. So, that was a very good preparation for me before I fully incarnated here with this avatar.

In the coming volumes, I will go into more details about some of my experiences and I will recount new ones. Particularly the ones I had with the Native Americans I encountered, some of whom I went on stage with, and also the Mongols of Huun Huur Tu with whom I spent a memorable evening, the Star Women from Siberia, etc. Obviously, I will also talk about my galactic contacts and about my hybrid children, Zarhya, Kalhynda, and Xie'Hon of the Yahyel nation, and about my meetings with several representatives of the star nations and the close ties I have with some of them. I will also recount the actions I have taken with others in the field, especially in Germany. Actions in the fourth dimension and even in a parallel universe, and how I came to create galactic portraits.

I will also discuss the secret space programs, to provide a bit more information. By the way, everything is linked and I think that my involvement in such programs is a direct result of my abductions. As a result, they enlisted me—with my consent—for a period of twenty years. At the end of the twenty-year period, they asked me if I would continue. I clearly told them I would not. So, they blocked my memory with implants and took me back in time. It may sound crazy, but that is what happened. They have a technological lead that you could not possibly imagine. Interplanetary travel, jumps in what I call "quantum mirrors," time displacement, body regeneration thanks to medipods, and so on … Our so-called modern society has no idea of what is going on behind the scenes, unbeknown to almost everyone.

But times are changing. As I write these lines, we have come out of global lock down. Under the cover of COVID19, a great deal has happened. Things that have to do with the Earth's liberation. There have also been great waves of energy coming from the Great Central Sun, some awareness in some people during this so-called pandemic. To me, and this is just me, it is all fear-mongering propaganda by the deep state to maintain control and power. Except that the game has turned against them. They are increasingly backed to the wall. The Reptilians and

Archons who still do not want to evolve and refuse love, have become trapped in their artificial matrix. In short, everything has accelerated. Much more than some would have you believe. So get ready for a paradigm shift, a life shift. For life as you have known it up to now is going to be turned upside down and be completely transformed. Get ready to enter this new cycle of evolution and ascension, for it is already upon us.

I will end this first volume by closing the circle with the one that began when I chose to come down to Earth, and which I used as my introduction.

Far, Far Away in the Galaxy ...

"Now, Kie'Teir, are you sure you want to incarnate with an avatar in this life sphere that Planet Earth is?"

"Definitely. It is a choice I thought through."

"Are you aware of the hardships you will have to face?"

"Never before have I had an experience like this on such a life sphere, so I do not really know what these concepts of 'separation,' ' fear,' 'suffering,' 'unease,' or 'solitude' are. In fact, the only thing that puzzles me, if I may say, is 'death' ... I cannot comprehend the notion of ceasing to live forever. We know that it is impossible, yet human beings are sure it is so. In any case, my soul wishes to 'go down' and experience all this, to bring my light to contribute in my own way to the change in consciousness."

"When you are there, limited by the envelope of this avatar and wondering what you are doing in this place, 'you will understand' ... From this state of consciousness in which you have always been until now, you cannot even guess what it is to experience density and limitation."

"I'll take up the challenge ... My choice has been made."

"So, if this is your will, I can only wish you a safe journey into the three-dimensional world and 'remind you' that we will be by your side observing and guiding you from this dimension. If you can open your heart wide enough—a task which is not easy at all, as you will see—you will be able 'to listen to us' and perceive our presence."

"And what is the best way to open the heart?"

"Observe what is going on inside. Listen to your inner voice. Take it easy and let go of the resistance to the fact that things on Earth are not the way you wish. Accept yourself as you are. It is the only way you will be able to accept others and honor their experiences. The peace and love which will be reborn in you following this acceptance will put you automatically 'in touch' with us."

"All right, I will keep it in mind."

"No, son ... You are going to forget. Those are the 'rules.' You will have to remember this while your physical body is already contaminated by judgments, attachments, and negative beliefs and is growing into adulthood. The light of your soul must emerge from the darkness of fear, mistrust, and misunderstanding. Trust, beloved. We are certain you will manage. Because you actually already have."

Out of the left hand of my father emerged a holographic projection with three spheres.

"What's this?"

"It is your human mother's womb. And this little embryo you can see inside is the avatar you are going to incarnate with."

"Yes, everything is planned. I have arranged with the soul who will travel with this body ... It will 'make way' for me when it has reached six Earth years."

"Have a good trip, stellar soul! Have a good trip, son!"

"Good-bye, Father!"

"The love of Source is with you. We love you."

A Last Short Note

Dear Starseeds, lightworkers and warriors, Blue Stars and Indigos, this is a fantastic time and you have chosen to be here, right now, during humanity's global awakening process. So, take part in it and place yourselves in the heart of the event.

Your love and energy are needed for the success of this great evolution/ascension.

"… and when the great Phoenix flies freely, look closely at what it will tenderly carry in its clutches. It will be a new green leaf, not from an olive branch, but from the new growth of the Sacred Tree, which will stand straight and strong again in the Circle of the new Nation of Humanity."

—No-Eyes[25]

25   Excerpt from Mary Summer Rain's Phoenix Rising, No-Eyes Vision of the Changes to Come (Hampton Roads Publishing Co., 1987).

Epilogue

All good things must come to an end and we have come to the end of this first volume of my series of books entitled Beyond Our World. This first volume covered the 1979–1996 period. This time was very telling but also full of surprises, joys, discomforts, torments, and above all, full of love.

I hope that you will have had as much pleasure reading it as I had writing it. Besides, if someone had told me a few years ago that I would write my story and share my experience with you one day, I would not have believed it. But then again, the ways of spirit, or of our soul, are sometimes mysterious. They create synchronicities which make us take one path rather than another. And from this direction we take, from these roads we walk, other synchronicities are created, through encounters, events, realizations, and choices. And even if we do create our lives, there are still a good many mysterious things. And that is just fine as it is. Because if we knew everything in advance, where would the fun be?

The goal is to be in the present moment, without worrying about the future, and to enjoy each moment by being fully who we really are. This is the most precious gift we can offer ourselves. Before being with this avatar, this human being with a third-dimensional identity, which is an illusion, we are souls. Souls which experience who they are until they remember who they really are, and therefore become a greater version of who they are. Such is the soul's will.

To fully express who it is through all these experiences in order to sense, feel, and live what it is. Only. And what it is, is Love. For we are pure love. Even if it is difficult for many to remember this, caught as they are in the illusion of this 3D matrix and all its prefabricated, preconceived patterns where everything is formatted. Hence the importance of refocusing fully. Of placing oneself in the heart, because our truth lies there and nowhere else. Do not look outside for answers to the many questions you may have, because everything is within you. What is called spiritual awakening will not happen thanks to someone else. No one can help you to awaken. The awakening occurs through awareness and reminders provided by your soul itself.

Other people can guide you, accompany you on your path, but in no way can they make you awaken. Anyone who claims otherwise does not measure the impact and power of his ego, in my opinion, and in most cases, the lure of profit and power. This is not a judgment, just an observation. I have personally seen people I knew who only swore by so-and-so and who were convinced that these people had "the Knowledge," that they held "the Truth," and that they alone could make them evolve. You always need discernment. Especially in spiritual milieus and currents, where you see all kinds of people who are there only for their personal profit and who use and abuse your good heart and your wallet.

For example, many people have asked me about my shamanic faculties in the past: "Why don't you set up shop? Why don't you open a practice and do shamanic healing? Why don't you set up shamanic courses?"

Why not? For one simple reason: I am not interested in this. Hard as this may be to believe, I have never been interested. I don't want to make a business out of it. These exchanges, sharing, caring, and singing are done in the heart and through the heart. I have always shown wisdom and humility. This shamanic aspect is an integral part of my true self, it is in my genes and in my Amerindian/Pleiadian descent DNA.

What's more, we are all born shamans, we don't become shamans. It's just that we have forgotten that. Everyone can be a Little Hollow Bone, that is to say a channel, a tube through which the other dimensions are accessible. And we become a Little Hollow Bone again the moment we are fully aligned and centered, as one with the world around us. The symbol of the Native American medicine wheel is the best tool to demonstrate this. It reminds you that the center is the key. Many people talk about only the four directions, but did you know that there are actually seven of them?

There is the East, South, West, and North, obviously, but there is also Mother Earth under our feet, Father Sky above us, and the last one is the Heart. Our heart. That is what the Great Whole contains. You cannot be complete unless you are fully aware of this. Because we are part of this Great Whole as the Great Whole is part of us. The microcosm within the macrocosm. As you become aware of this, you open up again to unity and oneness, knowing and understanding that everything is linked and that we are all connected and, I would even say, interconnected. Are we not all One?

As the Lakota say: "There is no 'I,' there is 'We.'"

And I would like to conclude with this: "A'Ho! Mitakuye oyasin!"

With love,
David Rousseau/Kie'Teir

About the Author

David Rousseau is a French-Irish-Native American, author of the books Beyond Our World, artist, singer, musician, and composer. Experiencer, empath, and contactee. At the age of six, he underwent abductions which attracted the attention of the French Secret Space Programs. He was then recruited at the age of eight for his exceptional psychic and intuitive abilities. He met Jean-Charles Moyen, then age twelve, on board the Solaris ship of the "Solar Warden" program.

At the end of his first twenty-year mission, he was rejuvenated and returned to the starting point in 1981.

He then signed up again for two more twenty-year missions.

He received the following honors: Appointed on July 13, 2021, as Universal Ambassador for Peace by the Universal Circle of Ambassadors for Peace of Paris/Geneva (France/Switzerland).

Illustration of me as Kie'Teir (right) when I chose to descend
to Earth. Copyright ©2020 Davian Art

This illustration shows my first meeting with Ezahyel at the age of six, and was used as the cover for this book in French

Abduction by the Greys of Orion. That day I was struggling because I no longer appreciated their way of doing things.

Encounter with Men in Black in Nantes, while Fabrice and I
were on our way to a meeting of ufologists.

With Ezahyel aboard his ship.

Representation of the being that appeared floating above the high school in the late 80s, early 90s.
Copyright ©2020 Davian Art

Representation of the armed commando who threatened me
one evening in an alley in Nantes.
Copyright ©2020 Davian Art

Meeting with the agent who tried to enlist me in a special
agency. Copyright ©2020 Davian Art

Ptesáŋwiŋ - White Buffalo Woman - is my mother in the Pleiades. She's been with me ever since. Copyright ©2020 Davian Art

Reunion and exchange with my mother Ptesáŋwiŋ. These moments will always be engraved in my memory.

This illustration represents the moment when I arrived in the Secret Space Programs at the age of eight. The exchanges between this soldier and the Greys were quite tense.
Copyright ©2020 Davian Art

Zarhya and Kalhynda, from the YAHYEL nation. These are my daughters, the result of hybridization during my abductions by the Greys.
Copyright ©2020 Davian Art

With Ezahyel and Xaman'Ek in a Martian base.
Copyright ©2020 Davian Art

The ancient Mayans as I saw them.
Copyright ©2020 Davian Art

The Reptilian Dracos that was in the underground base when
I arrived in the S.S.P.
Copyright ©2020 Davian Art

Ezahyel using healing energies. Healing energies are very powerful within him.
Copyright ©2020 Davian Art

Other Books by Ozark Mountain Publishing, Inc.

Dolores Cannon
A Soul Remembers Hiroshima
Between Death and Life
Conversations with Nostradamus,
    Volume I, II, III
The Convoluted Universe -Book One,
    Two, Three, Four, Five
The Custodians
Five Lives Remembered
Horns of the Goddess
Jesus and the Essenes
Keepers of the Garden
Legacy from the Stars
The Legend of Starcrash
The Search for Hidden Sacred
    Knowledge
They Walked with Jesus
The Three Waves of Volunteers and the
    New Earth
A Very Special Friend
Aron Abrahamsen
Holiday in Heaven
James Ream Adams
Little Steps
Justine Alessi & M. E. McMillan
Rebirth of the Oracle
Kathryn Andries
Time: The Second Secret
Will Alexander
Call Me Jonah
Cat Baldwin
Divine Gifts of Healing
The Forgiveness Workshop
Penny Barron
The Oracle of UR
P.E. Berg & Amanda Hemmingsen
The Birthmark Scar
Dan Bird
Finding Your Way in the Spiritual Age
Waking Up in the Spiritual Age
Julia Cannon
Soul Speak – The Language of Your
    Body
Jack Cauley
Journey for Life
Ronald Chapman
Seeing True
Jack Churchward
Lifting the Veil on the Lost
    Continent of Mu

The Stone Tablets of Mu
Carolyn Greer Daly
Opening to Fullness of Spirit
Patrick De Haan
The Alien Handbook
Paulinne Delcour-Min
Divine Fire
Holly Ice
Spiritual Gold
Anthony DeNino
The Power of Giving and Gratitude
Joanne DiMaggio
Edgar Cayce and the Unfulfilled
    Destiny of Thomas Jefferson
    Reborn
Paul Fisher
Like a River to the Sea
Anita Holmes
Twidders
Aaron Hoopes
Reconnecting to the Earth
Edin Huskovic
God is a Woman
Patricia Irvine
In Light and In Shade
Kevin Killen
Ghosts and Me
Susan Linville
Blessings from Agnes
Donna Lynn
From Fear to Love
Curt Melliger
Heaven Here on Earth
Where the Weeds Grow
Henry Michaelson
And Jesus Said – A Conversation
Andy Myers
Not Your Average Angel Book
Holly Nadler
The Hobo Diaries
Guy Needler
The Anne Dialogues
Avoiding Karma
Beyond the Source – Book 1, Book 2
The Curators
The History of God
The OM
The Origin Speaks

For more information about any of the above titles, soon to be released titles,
or other items in our catalog, write, phone or visit our website:
PO Box 754, Huntsville, AR 72740|479-738-2348/800-935-0045|www.ozarkmt.com

Other Books by Ozark Mountain Publishing, Inc.

Psycho Spiritual Healing
James Nussbaumer
And Then I Knew My Abundance
Each of You
Living Your Dram, Not Someone Else's
The Master of Everything
Mastering Your Own Spiritual Freedom
Sherry O'Brian
Peaks and Valley's
Gabrielle Orr
Akashic Records: One True Love
Let Miracles Happen
Nikki Pattillo
Children of the Stars
A Golden Compass
Victoria Pendragon
Being In A Body
Sleep Magic
The Sleeping Phoenix
Alexander Quinn
Starseeds What's It All About
Debra Rayburn
Let's Get Natural with Herbs
Charmian Redwood
A New Earth Rising
Coming Home to Lemuria
David Rousseau
Beyond Our World, Book 1
Richard Rowe
Exploring the Divine Library
Imagining the Unimaginable
Garnet Schulhauser
Dance of Eternal Rapture
Dance of Heavenly Bliss
Dancing Forever with Spirit
Dancing on a Stamp
Dancing with Angels in Heaven
Annie Stillwater Gray
The Dawn Book
Education of a Guardian Angel
Joys of a Guardian Angel
Work of a Guardian Angel
Manuella Stoerzer

Headless Chicken
Blair Styra
Don't Change the Channel
Who Catharted
Natalie Sudman
Application of Impossible Things
L.R. Sumpter
Judy's Story
The Old is New
We Are the Creators
Artur Tradevosyan
Croton
Croton II
Jim Thomas
Tales from the Trance
Jolene and Jason Tierney
A Quest of Transcendence
Paul Travers
Dancing with the Mountains
Nicholas Vesey
Living the Life-Force
Dennis Wheatley/ Maria Wheatley
The Essential Dowsing Guide
Maria Wheatley
Druidic Soul Star Astrology
Sherry Wilde
The Forgotten Promise
Lyn Willmott
A Small Book of Comfort
Beyond all Boundaries Book 1
Beyond all Boundaries Book 2
Beyond all Boundaries Book 3
D. Arthur Wilson
You Selfish Bastard
Stuart Wilson & Joanna Prentis
Atlantis and the New Consciousness
Beyond Limitations
The Essenes -Children of the Light
The Magdalene Version
Power of the Magdalene
Sally Wolf
Life of a Military Psychologist

For more information about any of the above titles, soon to be released titles,
or other items in our catalog, write, phone or visit our website:
PO Box 754, Huntsville, AR 72740|479-738-2348/800-935-0045|www.ozarkmt.com